Rhapsody

Rhapsody

A Dream Novel

Arthur Schnitzler

MINT EDITIONS

Rhapsody: A Dream Novel was first published in 1926.

This edition published by Mint Editions 2024.

ISBN 9798888975367 | E-ISBN 9798888975510

Published by Mint Editions®

 MINT
EDITIONS
minteditionbooks.com

Publishing Director: Katie Connolly
Design: Ponderosa Pine Design
Production and Project Management: Micaela Clark
Translated By: Otto P. Schinnerer
Typesetting: Westchester Publishing Services

Contents

I

Twenty-four brown-skinned slaves rowed the splendid galley which was to bring Prince Amgiad to the palace of the caliph. The Prince, wrapped in his purple cloak, lay alone on the deck under the dark-blue, starry sky, and his gaze—"

So far the little girl had read aloud. Then, suddenly, her eyelids drooped. Her parents looked at each other and smiled. Fridolin bent down, kissed her blonde hair and closed the book which was lying on the untidy table. The child looked up as if caught at some mischief.

"It's nine o'clock," her father said, "and time you were in bed." Albertina also bent over her, and as her hand met her husband's on the beloved forehead, they looked at each other with a tender smile not meant for the child. The governess entered and asked the little girl to say goodnight. She got up obediently, kissed her father and mother and walked out quietly hand in hand with the young woman.

Fridolin and Albertina, left alone under the reddish glow of the hanging-lamp, continued the conversation they had begun before supper.

It dealt with their experiences the night before at the masquerade ball. They had decided to attend it just before the end of the carnival period, as their first one of the season. No sooner had Fridolin entered the ballroom than he was greeted, like a long lost friend, by two women in red dominoes. He had no idea who they were, although they were unusually well-informed about many affairs of his student days and internship. They had invited him into a box with great friendliness, but had left again with the promise that they would soon return without masks. When they did not appear, he became impatient and went down to the ballroom floor hoping to meet them again, but eagerly as he scanned the room, he could not see them anywhere. Instead, however, another woman unexpectedly took his arm. It was his wife. She had just freed herself from the company of a stranger whose blasé manner and apparently Polish accent had at first charmed her. Suddenly he had offended her—frightened her by a rather common and impertinent remark. Fridolin and Albertina were glad to have escaped from a disappointingly commonplace masquerade prank, and soon sat like two lovers, among the other couples, in the buffet, eating oysters and drinking champagne. They chatted gaily, as though they had just made each other's acquaintance, acting a comedy of courting, bashful resistance, seduction and surrender.

After driving home quickly through the snowy winter night, they sank into each other's arms and were more blissful in their ardent love than they had been for a long time. The gray of morning awakened them only too soon. Fridolin's profession summoned him to his patients at an early hour, while Albertina would not stay in bed longer because of her duties as housewife and mother. So the ensuing hours passed, soberly and predetermined, in daily routine and work, and the events of the night before, both those at the beginning and at the end, had faded.

But now that the day's work was done—the child had gone to bed and no disturbance was likely—the shadowy forms of the masquerade, the melancholy stranger and the red dominoes, rose again into reality. And all at once those insignificant events were imbued, magically and painfully, with the deceptive glow of neglected opportunities. Harmless but probing questions, and sly, ambiguous answers were exchanged. Neither failed to notice that the other was not absolutely honest, and so they became slightly vindictive. They exaggerated the degree of attraction that their unknown partners at the ball had exerted upon them while each made fun of the other's tendencies to jealousy and denied his own. Soon, their light conversation about the trifling matters of the night before changed into a more serious discussion of those hidden, scarcely suspected wishes, which can produce dangerous whirlpools even in the serenest and purest soul. They spoke of those mysterious regions of which they were hardly conscious but toward which the incomprehensible wind of fate might some day drive them, even if only in their dreams. For though they were united in thought and feeling, they knew that the preceding day had not been the first time that the spirit of adventure, freedom and danger had beckoned them.

Uneasy, and tormenting themselves, each sought with disingenuous curiosity to draw out confessions from the other. Anxiously, they searched within themselves for some indifferent fact, or trifling experience, which might express the inexpressible, and the honest confession of which might relieve them of the strain and the suspicion which were becoming unbearable.

Whether Albertina was more impatient, more honest or more kind-hearted of the two, it was she who first summoned the courage for a frank confession. She asked Fridolin in a rather uncertain voice whether he remembered the young man who—last summer at the seashore in Denmark—had been sitting one evening with two other officers at an adjoining table. He had received a telegram during dinner, whereupon he had hastily said "goodbye" to his friends.

Fridolin nodded. "What about him?" he asked.

"I'd already seen him in the morning," she replied, "as he was hurrying up the stairs in the hotel with his yellow handbag. He looked at me as he passed, but didn't stop until he had gone a few more steps. Then he turned and our eyes met. He didn't smile; in fact, it seemed to me that he scowled. I suppose I did the same, for I was very much stirred. That whole day I lay on the beach, lost in dreams. Had he called me—I thought—I could not have resisted. I thought I was ready for anything. I had practically resolved to give up you, the child, my future, and at the same time—if you can understand it?—you were dearer to me than ever. That same afternoon—surely you remember—we discussed many things very intimately, among others our common future, and our child. At sunset you and I were sitting on the balcony, when, down below on the beach, he passed without looking up. I was extremely thrilled to see him, but I stroked your forehead and kissed your hair, and my love for you was both sorrowful and compassionate. That evening at dinner I wore a white rose and you yourself said I was very beautiful. Perhaps it wasn't mere chance that the stranger and his friends sat near us. He didn't look at me, but I considered getting up, walking over to him and saying: Here I am, my beloved for whom I have waited—take me. At that moment the telegram was handed to him. He read it, turned pale, whispered a few words to the younger of the two officers—and glancing at me mysteriously he left the room."

"And then?" Fridolin asked dryly when she stopped.

"That is all. I remember that I woke the next morning with a restless anxiety. I don't know whether I was afraid that he had left or that he might still be there. But when he didn't appear at noon, I breathed a sigh of relief. Don't ask anymore, Fridolin. I've told you the whole truth. And you, too, had some sort of experience at the seashore—I know it."

Fridolin rose, walked up and down the room several times and then said: "You're right." He was standing at the window, his face in shadow and in a hoarse and slightly hostile voice he began: "In the morning, sometimes very early before you got up, I used to stroll along the beach, out beyond the town. Even at that hour the sun was always shining over the sea, bright and strong. Out there on the beach, as you know, were cottages, each one standing like a world in itself. Some had fenced-in gardens, others were surrounded only by the woods. The bathing-huts were separated from the cottages by the road and part of the beach. I hardly ever met people at such an early hour, and bathers were never out. One morning, quite suddenly, I noticed the figure of a woman. She had suddenly appeared on the narrow ledge of a bathing-hut, which rested on piles driven into the sand. She was cautiously advancing, placing one foot before the other, her arms extended backward against the wooden boards. She was quite a young girl, possibly fifteen years old, with loose blonde hair hanging over her shoulders and on one side over her delicate breast. She was looking down into the water and was slowly moving along the wall, her gaze lowered in the direction of the far corner. All at once she stopped opposite me and reached far back with her arms as though trying to secure a firmer hold. Looking up, she suddenly saw me. A tremor passed through her body, as though she wished to drop into the water or run. But as she could move only very slowly on the narrow ledge, she had to stay where she was. She stood there with a face expressing at first fright, then anger, and finally embarrassment. All at once, however, she smiled, smiled marvelously. Her eyes welcomed me, beckoned to me, and at the same time slightly mocked me, as she glanced at the strip of water between us. Then she stretched her young and slender body, glad of her beauty, and proudly and sweetly stirred by my obvious admiration. We stood facing each other for perhaps ten seconds, with half-open lips and dazzled eyes. Involuntarily I stretched out my arms to her; her eyes expressed surrender and joy. Then she shook her head vigorously, took one arm from the wall and commanded me with a gesture to go away. When I didn't at once obey, her childlike eyes turned on me such a beseeching look that there was nothing for me to do but to go, and I went as quickly as possible. I did not look back once—not because I felt considerate, obedient or chivalrous, but because in her last glance I sensed an emotion so intense, so far beyond anything I had ever experienced, that I was not far from fainting." And he stopped.

With her eyes cast down and in a monotonous voice, Albertina asked: "And how often did you see her after that?"

"What I have told you," Fridolin answered, "happened on the last day of our stay in Denmark. Otherwise I don't know what might have taken place. You, too, mustn't ask any more, Albertina."

He was still standing at the window, motionless as Albertina arose and walked over to him. There were tears in her eyes and a slight frown on her face. "In the future let's always tell each other such things at once," she said.

He nodded in silence.

"Will you promise me?"

He took her into his arms. "Don't you know that?" he asked. But his voice was still harsh.

She took his hands and looked up at him with misty eyes, in the depths of which he could read her thoughts. She was thinking of his other and more real experiences, those of his young manhood, many of which she knew about. When they were first married he had yielded, all too readily, to her jealous curiosity and had told her (indeed it often seemed to him) had surrendered to her many secrets which he should rather have kept to himself. He knew that she was inevitably reminded of these affairs and he was hardly surprised when she murmured the half-forgotten name of one of his early sweethearts. It sounded to him a little like a reproach, or was it a covert threat?

He raised her hands to his lips.

"You may believe me, even though it sounds trite, that in every woman I thought I loved it was always you I was looking for—I know that better than you can understand it, Albertina."

A dispirited smile passed over her face. "And suppose before meeting you, I, too, had gone on a search for a mate?" she asked. The look in her eyes changed, becoming cool and impenetrable, and he allowed her hands to slip from his, as though he had caught her lying or committing a breach of faith. She, however, continued:

"Oh, if you men *knew*!" and again was silent.

"If we knew—? What do you mean by that?"

In a strangely harsh voice she replied: "About what you imagine, my dear."

"Albertina!—Then there is something that you've kept from me?"

She nodded, and looked down with a strange smile. Incomprehensible, monstrous doubts crossed his mind.

"I don't quite understand," he said. "You were barely seventeen when we became engaged."

"Past sixteen, yes, Fridolin. But it wasn't my fault that I was a virgin when I became your wife." She looked at him brightly.

"Albertina—!"

But she continued:

"It was a beautiful summer evening at Lake Wörther, just before our engagement, and a very handsome young man stood before my window that overlooked a large and spacious meadow. As we talked I thought to myself—just listen to this—what a charming young man that is—he would only have to say the word—it would have to be the right one, certainly—and I would go out with him into the meadow or the woods—or it would be even more beautiful in a boat on the lake—and I would grant him this night anything he might desire. That is what I thought to myself.—But he didn't say a word, that charming young man. He only kissed my hand tenderly—and next morning he asked me—if I would be his wife. And I said yes."

Fridolin was annoyed and dropped her hand. "And if," he said, "someone else had stood by your window that night and the right word had occurred to him, if it had been, for instance—" He was considering, but she raised her hand protestingly.

"Any other man—no matter who—could have said anything he liked—it would have been useless. And if it hadn't been you standing by the window, then very likely the summer evening wouldn't have been so beautiful." And she smiled at him.

There was a scornful expression about his mouth. "Yes, that's what you say now. Perhaps you even believe it at this moment. But—"

There was a knock on the door. The maid entered and said that the housekeeper from Schreyvogel Strasse had come to fetch the doctor, as the Privy Councilor was very low again. Fridolin went out into the hall, and when the woman told him that the Councilor had had a very serious heart attack, he promised to come at once.

As he was leaving, Albertina asked: "You're going away?" She said it with as much annoyance as if he were deliberately doing her an injustice.

Fridolin replied, with astonishment: "I suppose I've got to."

She sighed regretfully.

"I hope it won't be very serious," said Fridolin. "Up to now three centigrams of morphine have always pulled him through."

The maid brought his fur coat, and absentmindedly kissing Albertina on her forehead and mouth, as if everything during the last hour had been completely forgotten, he hurried away.

II

When Fridolin reached the street, he unbuttoned his coat. It had suddenly begun to thaw; the snow on the sidewalk was almost gone, and there was a touch of spring in the air. It was less than a quarter of an hour's walk to Schreyvogel Strasse from his home near the General Hospital, and he soon reached the old house. He walked up the dimly lighted winding staircase to the second floor and pulled the bell-rope. But before the old-fashioned bell was heard, he noticed that the door was ajar, and entering through the unlighted foyer into the living room he saw at once that he had come too late. The green-shaded kerosene lamp which was hanging from the low ceiling cast a dim light on the bedspread under which a lean body lay motionless. Fridolin knew the old man so well that he seemed to see the face plainly, although it was outside the circle of light—the high forehead, the thin and lined cheeks, the snow-white beard and also the strikingly ugly ears with coarse, white hairs. At the foot of the bed sat Marianne, the Councilor's daughter, completely exhausted, her arms hanging limply from her shoulders. An odor of old furniture, medicine, petroleum and cooking pervaded the room, and in addition to that there was a trace of eau de Cologne and scented soap. Fridolin also noticed the indefinite, sweetish scent of this pale girl who was still young and who had been slowly fading for months and years under the stress of severe household duties, nursing and night watches.

When the doctor entered she looked up, but because of the dim light he could not see whether she had blushed, as usual, when he appeared. She started to rise, but he stopped her with a movement of his hand, and so she merely greeted him with a nod, her eyes large and sad. He stepped to the head of the bed and mechanically placed his hands on the forehead of the dead man and on the arms which were lying on the bed-spread in loose and open shirt sleeves. His shoulders drooped with a slight expression of regret. He stuck his hands into the pockets of his coat and his eyes wandered about the room until they finally rested on Marianne. Her hair was blonde and thick, but dry; her neck well-formed and slender, although a little wrinkled and rather yellow; and her lips were thin and firmly pressed together.

"Well, my dear Marianne," he said in a slightly embarrassed whisper, "you weren't entirely unprepared for this."

She held out her hand to him. He took it sympathetically and inquired about the particulars of the final, fatal attack. She reported briefly and to the point, and then spoke of her father's last comparatively easy days, during which Fridolin had not seen him. Drawing up a chair, he sat down opposite her, and tried to console her by saying that her father must have suffered very little at the last. He then asked if any of her relatives had been notified. Yes, she said, the housekeeper had already gone to tell her uncle, and very likely Doctor Roediger would soon appear. "My fiancé," she added, and did not look him straight in the eye.

Fridolin simply nodded. During the year he had met Doctor Roediger two or three times in the Councilor's house. The pale young man—an instructor in History at the University of Vienna—was of an unusually slender build with a short, blond beard and spectacles, and had made quite a good impression upon him, without, however, arousing his interest beyond that. Marianne would certainly look better, he thought to himself, if she were his mistress. Her hair would be less dry, her lips would be fuller and redder. I wonder how old she is, he reflected. The first time I attended the Councilor, three or four years ago, she was twenty-three. At that time her mother was still living and she was more cheerful than now. She even took singing lessons for a while. So she is going to marry this instructor! I wonder why? She surely isn't in love with him, and he isn't likely to have much money either. What kind of a marriage will it turn out to be? Probably like a thousand others. But it's none of my business. It's quite possible that I shall never see her again, since there's nothing more for me to do here. Well, many others that I cared for have gone the same way.

As these thoughts passed through his mind, Marianne began to speak of her father—with fervor—as if his death had suddenly made him a more remarkable person. Then he was really only fifty-four years old? Well, of course, he had had so many worries and disappointments—his wife always ill—and his son such a grief! What, she had a brother? Certainly, she had once told the doctor about him. Her brother was now living somewhere abroad. A picture that he had painted when he was fifteen was hanging over there in Marianne's room. It represented an officer galloping down a hill. Her father had always pretended not to see it although it wasn't bad. Oh yes, if he'd had a chance her brother might have made something of himself.

How excitedly she speaks, Fridolin thought, and how bright her eyes are! Is it fever? Quite possibly. She's grown much thinner. Probably has tuberculosis.

She kept up her stream of talk, but it seemed to him that she didn't quite know what she was saying. It was twelve years since her brother had left home. In fact, she had been a child when he disappeared. They had last heard from him four or five years ago, at Christmas, from a small city in Italy. Strange to say, she had forgotten the name. She continued like this for a while, almost incoherently. Suddenly she stopped and sat there silently, her head resting in her hands. Fridolin was tired and even more bored. He was anxiously waiting for someone to come, her relatives, or her fiancé. The silence in the room was oppressive. It seemed to him that the dead man joined in the silence, deliberately and with malicious joy.

With a side glance at the corpse, he said: "At any rate, Fräulein Marianne, as things are now, it is fortunate that you won't have to stay in this house very much longer." And when she raised her head a little, without, however, looking at Fridolin, he continued: "I suppose your fiancé will soon get a professorship. The chances for promotion are more favorable in the Faculty of Philosophy than with us in Medicine." He was thinking that, years ago, he also had aspired to an academic career, but because he wanted a comfortable income, he had finally decided to practice medicine. Suddenly he felt that compared with this noble Doctor Roediger, he was the inferior.

"We shall move soon," said Marianne listlessly, "he has a post at the University of Göttingen."

"Oh," said Fridolin, and was about to congratulate her but it seemed rather out of place at the moment. He glanced at the closed window, and without asking for permission but availing himself of his privilege as a doctor, he opened both casements and let some air in. It had become even warmer and more spring-like, and the breeze seemed to bring with it a slight fragrance of the distant awakening woods. When he turned back into the room, he saw Marianne's eyes fixed upon him with a questioning look. He moved nearer to her and said: "I hope the fresh air will be good for you. It has become quite warm, and last night"— he was about to say: we drove home from the masquerade in a snowstorm, but he quickly changed the sentence and continued: "Last night the snow was still lying on the streets a foot and a half deep."

She hardly heard what he said. Her eyes became moist, large tears streamed down her cheeks and again she buried her face in her hands. In spite of himself, he placed his hand on her head, caressing it. He could feel her body beginning to tremble, and her sobs which were at first very quiet, gradually became louder and finally quite unrestrained. All at once she slipped down from her chair and lay at Fridolin's feet, clasping his knees with her arms and pressing her face against them. Then she looked up to him with large eyes, wild with grief, and whispered ardently: "I don't want to leave here. Even if you never return, if I am never to see you again, I want, at least, to live near you."

He was touched rather than surprised, for he had always known that she either was, or imagined herself to be, in love with him.

"Please—get up, Marianne," he said softly and bending down he gently raised her. Of course, she is hysterical, he remarked to himself and he glanced at her dead father. I wonder if he hears everything, he thought. Perhaps he isn't really dead. Perhaps everyone in the first hours after passing away, is only in a coma. He put his arms about her in a very hesitating embrace, and almost against his will he kissed her on the forehead, an act that somehow seemed rather ridiculous. He had a fleeting recollection of reading a novel years ago in which a young man, still almost a boy, had been seduced, in fact, practically raped, by the friend of his mother at the latter's deathbed. At the same time he thought of his wife, without knowing why, and he was conscious of some bitterness and a vague animosity against the man with the yellow handbag on the hotel stairs in Denmark. He held Marianne closer, but without the slightest emotion. The sight of her lustreless, dry hair, the indefinite, sweetish scent of her unaired dress gave him a slight feeling of revulsion. The bell outside rang again, and feeling he was released, he hastily kissed Marianne's hand, as if in gratitude, and went to open the door. Doctor Roediger stood there, in a dark gray top coat, an umbrella in his hand and a serious face, appropriate to the occasion. The two men greeted each other much more cordially than was called for by their actual state of acquaintance. Then they stepped into the room. After an embarrassed look at the deceased, Roediger expressed his sympathy to Marianne, while Fridolin went into the adjoining room to write out the official death-certificate. He turned up the gaslight over the desk and his eyes fell upon the picture of the white-uniformed officer, galloping down hill, with drawn sabre, to meet an invisible enemy. It hung in a narrow frame of dull gold and rather resembled a modest chromo-lithograph.

With his death-certificate filled out, Fridolin returned to the room where the engaged couple sat, hand in hand, by the bed of the dead Councilor.

Again the doorbell rang and Doctor Roediger rose to answer it. While he was gone, Marianne, with her eyes on the floor, said, almost inaudibly: "I love you," and Fridolin answered by pronouncing her name tenderly. Then Roediger came back with an elderly couple, Marianne's uncle and aunt, and a few words, appropriate to the occasion, were exchanged, with the usual embarrassment in the presence of one who has just died. The little room suddenly seemed crowded with mourners. Fridolin felt superfluous, took his leave and was escorted to the door by Roediger who said a few words of gratitude and expressed the hope of seeing him soon again.

III

When Fridolin stood on the street in front of the house, he looked up at the window which he himself had opened a little while before. The casements were swaying slightly in the wind of early spring, and the people who remained behind them up there, the living as well as the dead, all seemed unreal and phantomlike. He felt as if he had escaped from something, not so much from an adventure, but rather from a melancholy spell the power of which he was trying to break. He felt strangely disinclined to go home. The snow in the streets had melted, except where little heaps of dirty white had been piled up on either side of the curb. The gas-flame in the street lamps flickered and a nearby church bell struck eleven. Fridolin decided that before going to bed, he would spend a half hour in a quiet nook of a café near his residence. As he walked through Rathaus Park he noticed here and there on benches standing in the shadow, that couples were sitting, clasped together, just as if Spring had actually arrived and no danger were lurking in the deceptive, warm air. A tramp in tattered clothes was lying full length on a bench with his hat over his face. Suppose I wake him and give him some money for a night's lodging, Fridolin thought. But what good would that do? Then I would have to provide for the next night, too, or there'd be no sense in it, and in the end I might be suspected of having criminal relations with him. He quickened his steps to escape as rapidly as possible from all responsibility and temptation. And why only this one? He asked himself. There are thousands of such poor devils in Vienna alone. It's manifestly impossible to help all of them or to worry about all the poor wretches! He was reminded of the dead man he had just left, and shuddered; in fact, he felt slightly nauseated at the thought that decay and decomposition, according to eternal laws, had already begun their work in the lean body under the brown flannel blanket. He was glad that he was still alive, and in all probability these ugly things were still far removed from him. He was, in fact, still in the prime of youth, he had a charming and lovable wife and could have several women in addition, if he happened to want them, although, to be sure, such affairs required more leisure than was his. He then remembered that he would have to be in his ward at the hospital at eight in the morning, visit his private patients from eleven to one, keep office hours from three to five, and that even in the evening he had several appointments to visit patients. Well, he hoped that it would be sometime before he would again be called out so late at night. As he crossed Rathaus Square, which had a dull gleam like a brownish pond, and turned homeward, he heard the muffled sound of marching steps in the distance. Then he saw, still quite far away, a small group of fraternity students, six or eight in number, turning a corner and coming towards him. When the light of a street lamp fell upon them he thought he recognized them, with their blue caps, as members of the *Alemannia*, for although he had never belonged to a fraternity, he had fought a few sabre duels in his time. In thinking of his student days he was reminded again of the red dominoes who had lured him into a box at the ball the night before and then had so shamefully deserted him. The students were quite near now; they were laughing and talking loudly. Perhaps one or two of them were from the hospital? But it was impossible to see their faces plainly because of the dim light, and he had to stay quite close to the houses so as not to collide with them. Now they had passed. Only the one in the rear, a tall fellow with open overcoat and a bandage over his left eye, seemed to lag behind, and deliberately bumped into him with his raised elbow. It couldn't have been mere chance. What's got into that fellow? Fridolin thought, and involuntarily he stopped. The other took two more steps and turned. They looked at each other for a moment with only a short distance separating them. Suddenly Fridolin turned around again and went on. He heard a short laugh behind him and he longed to challenge the fellow, but he felt his heart beating strangely, just as it had on a previous occasion, twelve or fourteen years before. There had been an unusually loud knock on his door while he had had with him a certain charming young creature who was never tired of prattling about her jealous fiancé. As a matter of fact, it was only the postman who had knocked in such a threatening manner. And now he felt his heart beating just as it had at that time.

What's the meaning of this? he asked himself, and he noticed that his knees were shaking a little. Am I a coward? Oh! Nonsense, he reassured himself. Why should I go and face a drunken student, I, a man of thirty-five, a practising physician, a married man and father of a child? Formal challenge! Seconds! A duel! And perhaps because of such a silly encounter receive a cut in my arm and be unable to perform my professional duties?—Or lose an eye?—Or even get blood-poisoning?—And in a week perhaps be in the same position as the man in Schreyvogel Strasse under the brown flannel blanket? Coward—? He had fought three sabre duels, and had even been ready to fight a duel with pistols, and it wasn't at *his* request that the matter had been called off. And what about his profession! There were dangers lurking everywhere and at all times—except that one usually forgets about them. Why, how long ago was it that that child with diphtheria had coughed in his face? Only three or four days, that's all. After all, that was much more dangerous than a little fencing match with sabres, and he hadn't given it a second thought. Well, if he ever met that fellow again, the affair could still be straightened out. He was by no means bound by the code of honor to take a silly encounter with a student seriously when on an errand of mercy, to or from a patient. But if, for instance, he should meet the young Dane with whom Albertina—oh, nonsense, what was he thinking of? Well, after all, it was just as bad as if she had been his mistress. Even worse. Yes, just let that fellow cross his path! What a joy it would be to face him somewhere in a clearing in the woods and aim a pistol at his forehead with its smoothly combed blond hair.

He suddenly discovered that he had passed his destination. He was in a narrow street in which only a few doubtful-looking women were strolling about in a pitiful attempt to bag their game. It's phantomlike, he thought. And in retrospect the students, too, with their blue caps, suddenly seemed unreal. The same was true of Marianne, her fiancé, her uncle and aunt, all of whom he pictured standing hand in hand around the deathbed of the old Councilor. Albertina, too, whom he could see in his mind's eye soundly sleeping, her arms folded under her head—even his child lying in the narrow white brass bed, rolled up in a heap, and the red-cheeked governess with the mole on her left temple—all of them seemed to belong to another world. Although this idea made him shudder a bit, it also reassured him, for it seemed to free him from all responsibility, and to loosen all the bonds of human relationship.

One of the girls wandering about stopped him. She was still a young and pretty little thing, very pale with red-painted lips. She also might lead to a fatal end, only not as quickly, he thought. Is this cowardice too? I suppose really it is. He heard her steps and then her voice behind him. "Won't you come with me, doctor?"

He turned around involuntarily. "How do you know who I am?" he asked.

"Why, I don't know you," she said, "but here in this part of town they're all doctors, aren't they?"

He had had no relations with a woman of this sort since he had been a student at the *Gymnasium*. Was the attraction this girl had for him a sign that he was suddenly reverting to adolescence? He recalled a casual acquaintance, a smart young man, who was supposed to be extremely successful with women. Once while Fridolin was a student he had been sitting with him in an all-night café, after a ball. When the young man proposed to leave with one of the regular girls of the place, Fridolin looked at him in surprise. Thereupon he answered: "After all, it's the most convenient way—and they aren't by any means the worst."

"What's your name?" Fridolin asked the girl.

"Well, what do you think? Mizzi, of course." She unlocked the house-door, stepped into the hallway and waited for Fridolin to follow her.

"Come on," she said when he hesitated. He stepped in beside her, the door closed behind him, she locked it, lit a wax candle and went ahead, lighting the way.—Am I mad? He asked himself. Of course I shall have nothing to do with her.

An oil-lamp was burning in her room, and she turned it up. It was a fairly pleasant place and neatly kept. At any rate, it smelled fresher than Marianne's home, for instance. But then, of course,

ARTHUR SCHNITZLER

no old man had been lying ill there for months. The girl smiled, and without forwardness approached Fridolin who gently kept her at a distance. She pointed to a rocking-chair into which he was glad to drop.

"You must be very tired," she remarked. He nodded. Undressing without haste, she continued: "Well, no wonder, with all the things a man like you has to do in the course of a day. We have an easier time of it."

He noticed that her lips were not painted, as he had thought, but were a natural red, and he complimented her on that.

"But why should I rouge?" she inquired. "How old do you think I am?"

"Twenty?" Fridolin ventured.

"Seventeen," she said, and sat on his lap, putting her arms around his neck like a child.

Who in the world would suspect that I'm here in this room at this moment? Fridolin thought. I'd never have thought it possible an hour or even ten minutes ago. And—why? Why am I here? Her lips were seeking his, but he drew back his head. She looked at him with sad surprise and slipped down from his lap. He was sorry, for he had felt much comforting tenderness in her embrace.

She took a red dressing gown which was hanging over the foot of the open bed, slipped into it and folded her arms over her breast so that her entire body was concealed.

"Does this suit you better?" she asked without mockery, almost timidly, as though making an effort to understand him. He hardly knew what to answer.

"You're right," he said. "I am really tired, and I find it very pleasant sitting here in the rocking-chair and simply listening to you. You have such a nice gentle voice. Just talk to me."

She sat down on the couch and shook her head.

"You're simply afraid," she said softly—and then to herself in a barely audible voice: "It's too bad."

These last words made the blood race through his veins. He walked over to her, longing to touch her, and declared that he trusted her implicitly and saying so he spoke the truth. He put his arms around her and wooed her like a sweetheart, like a beloved woman, but she resisted, until he felt ashamed and finally gave it up.

She explained: "You never can tell, sometime or other it's bound to get out. It's quite right of you to be afraid. If something should happen, you would curse me."

She was so positive in refusing the banknotes which he offered her that he did not insist. She put a little blue woolen shawl about her shoulders, lit a candle to light him downstairs, went down with him and unlocked the door. "I'm not going out anymore tonight," she said. He took her hand and involuntarily kissed it. She looked up to him astonished, almost frightened. Then she laughed, embarrassed and happy. "Just as if I were a young lady," she said.

The door closed behind Fridolin and he quickly made a mental note of the street number, so as to be able to send the poor little thing some wine and cakes the following day.

IV

Meanwhile it had become even milder outside. A fragrance from dewy meadows and distant mountains drifted with the gentle breezes into the narrow street. Where shall I go now? Fridolin asked himself, as though it weren't the obvious thing to go home to bed. But he couldn't persuade himself to do so. He felt homeless, an outcast, since his annoying meeting with the students. . . or was it since Marianne's confession? No, it was longer than that—ever since this evening's conversation with Albertina he was moving farther and farther away from his everyday existence into some strange and distant world.

He wandered about aimlessly through the dark streets, letting the breeze blow through his hair. Finally, he turned resolutely into a third-rate coffeehouse. The place was dimly lighted and not especially large, but it had an old-fashioned, cozy air about it, and was almost empty at this late hour.

Three men were playing cards in a corner. The waiter who had been watching them helped Fridolin take off his fur coat, took his order and placed illustrated journals and evening papers on his table.

Fridolin felt slightly more secure and began to look through the papers. His eyes were arrested here and there by some news-item. In some Bohemian city, street signs with German names had been torn down. There was a conference in Constantinople in which Lord Cranford took part about constructing a railway in Asia Minor. The firm Benies & Weingruber had gone into bankruptcy. The prostitute Anna Tiger, in a fit of jealousy, had attempted to throw vitriol on her friend, Hermine Drobizky. An Ash Wednesday fish-dinner was being given that evening in Sophia Hall. Marie B., a young girl residing at No. 28 Schönbrunn Strasse, had poisoned herself with mercuric chloride.—Prosaically commonplace as they were, all these facts, the insignificant as well as the sad, had a sobering and reassuring effect on Fridolin. He felt sorry for the young girl, Marie B. How stupid to take mercuric chloride! At this very moment, while he was sitting snugly in the café, while Albertina was calmly sleeping, and the Councilor had passed beyond all human suffering, Marie B., No. 28 Schönbrunn Strasse, was writhing in incredible pain.

He looked up from his paper and encountered the gaze of a man seated opposite. Was it possible? Nachtigall—? The latter had already recognized him, threw up his hands in pleased surprise and joined him at his table. He was still a young man, tall, rather broad, and none too thin. His long, blond, slightly curly hair had a touch of gray in it, and his moustache drooped in Polish fashion. He was wearing an open gray top coat, underneath which were visible a greasy dress suit, a crumpled shirt with three false diamond studs, a crinkled collar and a dangling, white silk tie. His eyelids were inflamed, as if from many sleepless nights, but his blue eyes gleamed brightly.

"You here in Vienna, Nachtigall?" exclaimed Fridolin.

"Didn't you know?" said Nachtigall with a soft, Polish accent and a slightly Jewish twang. "How could you miss it, and me so famous?" He laughed loudly and good-naturedly, and sat down opposite Fridolin.

"What," asked Fridolin, "have you been appointed Professor of Surgery without my hearing of it?"

Nachtigall laughed still louder. "Didn't you hear me just now, just a minute ago?"

"What do you mean—hear you?—Why, of course." Suddenly it occurred to him that someone had been playing the piano when he entered; in fact, he had heard music coming from some basement as he approached the café. "So that was you playing?" he exclaimed.

"It was," Nachtigall said, laughing.

Fridolin nodded. Why, of course—the strangely vigorous touch, the peculiar, but euphonious bass chords had at once seemed familiar to him. "Are you devoting yourself entirely to it?" he asked. He remembered that Nachtigall had definitely given up the study of medicine after his second preliminary examination in zoology, which he had passed although he was seven years late in taking it. Since then he had been hanging around the hospital, the dissecting room, the laboratories and classrooms for sometime afterwards. With his blond artist's head, his crinkled collar, his dangling tie that had once been white, he had been a striking and, in the humorous sense, popular figure. He had been much liked, not only by his fellow-students, but also by many professors. The son of a Jewish gin-shop owner in a small Polish town, he had left home early and had come to Vienna to study medicine. The trifling sums he received from his parents had from the very-beginning been scarcely worth mention and were soon discontinued. However, this didn't prevent his appearing in the Riedhof Hotel at the table reserved for medical students where Fridolin was a regular guest. At intervals, one after another of his more well-to-do fellow-students would pay his bill. He sometimes, also, was given clothes, which he accepted gladly and without false pride. He had already learned to play in his home town from a pianist stranded there, and while he was a medical student in Vienna he had studied at the Conservatory where he was considered a talented musician of great promise. But here, too, he was neither serious nor diligent enough to develop his art systematically. He soon became entirely content with the impression he made on his acquaintances, or rather with the pleasure he gave them by his playing. For a while he had a position as pianist in a suburban dancing school.

Fellow-students and table-companions tried to introduce him into fashionable houses in the same capacity, but on such occasions he would play only what suited him and as long as he chose. His conversations with the young girls present were not always harmless, and he drank more than he could carry. Once, playing for a dance in the house of a wealthy banker, he embarrassed several couples with flattering but improper remarks, and ended up by playing a wild cancan and singing a risque song with his powerful, bass voice. The host gave him a severe calling down, but Nachtigall, blissfully hilarious, got up and embraced him. The latter was furious and, although himself a Jew, hurled a common insult at him. Nachtigall at once retaliated with a powerful box on his ears, and this definitely concluded his career in the fashionable houses of the city. He behaved better, on the whole, in more intimate circles, although sometimes when the hour was late, he had to be put out of the place by force. But the following morning all was forgiven and forgotten. One day, long after his friends had graduated, he disappeared from the city without a word. For a few months he sent post cards from various Russian and Polish cities, and once Fridolin, who was one of Nachtigall's favorites, was reminded of his existence not only by a card, but by a request for a moderate sum of money, without explanation. Fridolin sent it at once, but never received a word of thanks or any other sign of life from Nachtigall.

At this moment, however, eight years later, at a quarter to one in the morning, Nachtigall insisted on paying his debt, and took the exact amount in bank-notes from a rather shabby pocket-book. As the latter was fairly well filled, Fridolin accepted the repayment with a good conscience.

"Are you getting along well," he asked with a smile, in order to make sure.

"I can't complain," replied Nachtigall. Placing his hand on Fridolin's arm, he continued: "But tell me, why are you here so late at night?"

Fridolin explained that he had needed a cup of coffee after visiting a patient, although he didn't say, without quite knowing why, that he hadn't found his patient alive. Then he talked in very general terms of his duties at the hospital and his private practice, and mentioned that he was happily married, and the father of a six year old girl.

Nachtigall in his turn, explained that he had spent the time as a pianist in every possible sort of Polish, Roumanian, Serbian and Bulgarian city and town, just as Fridolin had surmised. He had a wife and four children living in Lemberg, and he laughed heartily, as though it were unusually jolly to have four children, all of them living in Lemberg, and all by one and the same woman. He had been back in Vienna since the preceding fall. The vaudeville company he had been with had suddenly gone to pieces. He was now playing anywhere and everywhere, anything that happened to come along, sometimes in two or three different houses the same night. For example, down there in that basement—not at all a fashionable place, as he remarked, really a sort of bowling alley, and with very doubtful patrons.

"But if you have to provide for four children and a wife in Lemberg"—he laughed again, though not quite as gaily as before, and added: "But sometimes I am privately engaged." Noticing a reminiscent smile on Fridolin's face, he continued: "Not just in the houses of bankers and such, but in all kinds of circles, even larger ones, both public and secret."

"Secret?" Fridolin asked.

Nachtigall looked straight before him with a gloomy and crafty air, and said: "They will be calling for me again in a minute."

"What, are you playing somewhere else tonight?"

"Yes, they only begin there at two."

"It must be an unusually smart place."

"Yes and no," said Nachtigall, laughing, but he became serious again at once.

"Yes and no?" queried Fridolin, curiously.

Nachtigall bent across the table.

"I'm playing tonight in a private house, but I don't know whose it is."

"Then you're playing there for the first time?" Fridolin asked with increasing interest.

"No, it's the third time, but it will probably be a different house again."

"I don't understand."

"Neither do I," said Nachtigall, laughing, "but you'd better not ask anymore."

"Oh, I see," remarked Fridolin.

"No, you're wrong. It's not what you think. I've seen a great deal in my time. It's unbelievable what one sees in such small towns, especially in Roumania, but here. . ." He drew back the yellow curtain from the window, looked out on the street and said as if to himself: "Not here yet." Then he turned to Fridolin and explained: "I mean the carriage. There's always a carriage to call for me, a different one each time."

"You're making me very curious, Nachtigall," Fridolin assured him.

"Listen to me," said Nachtigall after a slight pause. "I'd like to be able to arrange it—but how can I do it—" Suddenly he burst out: "Have you got plenty of nerve?"

"That's a strange question," said Fridolin in the tone of an offended fraternity student.

"I don't mean that."

"Well, what do you mean?—Why does one need so much courage for this affair? What can possibly happen?" He gave a short and contemptuous laugh.

"Nothing can happen to *me*. At best this would be the last time—but perhaps that may be the case anyhow." He stopped and looked out again through the crevice in the curtain.

"Well, then where's the difficulty?"

"What did you say?" asked Nachtigall, as if coming out of a dream.

"Tell me the rest of the story, now that you've started. A secret party? Closed affair? Nothing but invited guests?"

"I don't know. The last time there were thirty people, and the first time only sixteen."

"A ball?"

"Of course, a ball." He seemed to be sorry he had spoken of the matter at all.

"And you're furnishing the music for the occasion?"

"What do you mean—for the occasion? I don't know for what occasion. I simply play—with bandaged eyes."

"Nachtigall, what do you mean?"

Nachtigall sighed a little and continued: "Unfortunately my eyes are not completely bandaged, so that I can occasionally see something. I can see through the black silk handkerchief over my eyes in the mirror opposite." And he stopped.

"In other words," said Fridolin impatiently and contemptuously, but feeling strangely excited, "naked females."

"Don't say females," replied Nachtigall in an offended tone, "you never saw such women."

Fridolin hemmed and hawed a little. "And what's the price of admission?" he asked casually.

"Do you mean tickets and such? There are none."

"Well, how does one gain admittance?" asked Fridolin with compressed lips and tapping on the table with his fingers.

"You have to know the password, and it's a new one each time."

"And what's the one for tonight?"

"I don't know yet. I'll only find out from the coachman."

"Take me along, Nachtigall."

"Impossible. It's too dangerous."

"But a minute ago you yourself spoke. . . of being willing to. . . I think you can manage all right."

Nachtigall looked at him critically and said: "It would be absolutely impossible in your street clothes, for everyone is masked, men and women. As you haven't a masquerade outfit with you, it's out of the question. Perhaps the next time. I'll try to figure out some way." He listened attentively, peered again through the opening in the curtain and said with a sigh of relief: "There's my carriage, goodbye."

Fridolin hung on to his arm and said: "You can't get away that way. You've got to take me along."

"But my dear man. . ."

"Leave it to me. I know that it's dangerous. Perhaps that's the very thing that tempts me."

"But I've already told you—without costume and mask—"

"There are places to rent costumes."

"At one o'clock in the morning?"

"Listen here, Nachtigall. There's just such a place at the corner of Wickenburg Strasse. I walk past it several times a day." And he added, with growing excitement:

"You stay here for another quarter of an hour, Nachtigall. In the meantime I'll see what luck I have. The proprietor of the costume shop probably lives in the same building. If he doesn't— well, then I'll simply give it up for tonight. Let fate decide the question. There's a café in the same building. I think it's called Café Vindobona. You tell the coachman that you've forgotten something in the café, walk in, and I'll be waiting near the door. Then you can give me the password and get back into your carriage. If I manage to get a costume I'll take a cab and immediately follow you. The rest will take care of itself. I give you my word of honor, Nachtigall, that if you run any risk, I'll assume complete responsibility."

Nachtigall had tried several times to interrupt Fridolin, but it was useless—

The former threw some money on the table to pay his bill, including a generous tip which seemed appropriate for the style of the night, and left. A closed carriage was standing outside. A coachman dressed entirely in black with a tall silk hat, sat on the box, motionless. It looks like a mourning-coach, Fridolin thought. He ran down the street and reached the corner-house he was looking for a few minutes later. He rang the bell, inquired from the caretaker whether the costumer Gibiser lived in the house, and hoped in the bottom of his heart that he would receive a negative answer. But Gibiser actually lived there, on the floor below that of the costume shop. The caretaker did not seem especially surprised at having such a late caller. Made affable by Fridolin's liberal tip, he stated that it was not unusual during the carnival for people to come at such a late hour to hire costumes. He lighted the way from below with a candle until Fridolin had rung the bell on the second floor. Herr Gibiser himself opened the door for him, as if he had been waiting there. He was a bald-headed, haggard man and wore an old-fashioned, flowered dressing gown and a tasselled, Turkish cap which made him look like a foolish old man on the stage. Fridolin asked for a costume and said that the price did not matter, whereupon Herr Gibiser remarked, almost disdainfully: "I ask a fair price, no more."

He led the way up a winding staircase into the store. There was an odor of silk, velvet, perfume, dust and withered flowers, and a glitter of silver and red out of the indistinct darkness. A number of little electric bulbs suddenly shone between the open cabinets of a long, narrow passage, the end of which was enveloped in darkness. There were all kinds of costumes hanging to the right and to the left. On one side knights, squires, peasants, hunters, scholars, Orientals and clowns; on the other, ladies-at-court, baronesses, peasant women, lady's maids, queens of the night. The corresponding headdresses were on a shelf above the costumes. Fridolin felt as though he were walking through a gallery of hanged people who were on the point of asking each other to dance. Herr Gibiser followed him. Finally he asked: "Is there anything special you want? Louis Quatorze, Directoire, or Old-German?"

"I need a dark cassock and a black mask, that's all."

At this moment the clink of glasses rang out from the end of the passage. Fridolin was startled and looked at the costumer, as though he felt an explanation were due. Gibiser, however, merely groped for a switch which was concealed somewhere. A blinding light was diffused over the entire passage down to the end where a little table, covered with plates, glasses and bottles, could be seen. Two men, dressed in the red robes of vehmic judges, sprang up from two chairs beside the table and a graceful little girl disappeared at the same moment. Gibiser rushed forward with long strides, reached across the table and grabbed a white wig in his hand. Simultaneously a young and charming girl, still almost a child, wearing a Pierrette costume, wriggled out from under the table and ran along the passage to Fridolin who caught her in his arms. Gibiser dropped the white wig and grabbed the two vehmic judges by their robes. At the same time he called out to Fridolin: "Hold on to that girl for me." The child pressed against Fridolin as though sure of protection. Her little oval face was covered with powder and several beauty spots, and a fragrance of roses and powder arose from her delicate breasts. There was a smile of impish desire in her eyes.

"Gentlemen," cried Gibiser, "you will stay here while I call the police."

"What's got into you?" they exclaimed, and continued as if with one voice: "We were invited by the young lady."

Gibiser released his hold and Fridolin heard him saying: "You will have to explain this. Couldn't you see that the girl was deranged? Then turning to Fridolin, he said: "Sorry to keep you waiting."

"Oh, it doesn't matter," said Fridolin.

He would have liked to stay, or, better still, to take the girl with him, no matter where—and whatever the consequences. She looked up at him with alluring and child-like eyes, as if spellbound. The men at the end of the passage were arguing excitedly. Gibiser turned to Fridolin and asked in a matter-of-fact way: "You wanted a cassock, a pilgrim's hat and a mask?"

"No," said Pierrette with gleaming eyes, "you must give this gentleman a cloak lined with ermine and a doublet of red silk."

"Don't you budge from my side," answered Gibiser. Then he pointed to a dark frock hanging between a medieval soldier and a Venetian Senator, and said: "That's about your size and here's the hat. Take it quick."

The two strange men protested again: "You'll have to let us out at once, Herr Chibisier." Fridolin noticed with surprise the French pronunciation of the name Gibiser.

"That's out of the question," replied the costumer scornfully. "You'll kindly wait here until I return."

Meanwhile Fridolin slipped into the cassock and tied the white cords. Gibiser, who was standing on a narrow ladder, handed him the black, broad-rimmed pilgrim's hat, and he put it on. But he did all this unwillingly, being more and more convinced that danger was threatening Pierrette and that it was his duty to remain and help her. The mask which Gibiser gave him and which he at once tried on, smelt strange and rather disagreeable.

"You walk down ahead of me," Gibiser commanded the girl, pointing to the stairs. Pierrette turned and waved a gay, yet wistful farewell. Fridolin's eyes followed the direction of her gaze. The two men were no longer in costume but wore evening clothes and white ties, though their faces were still covered by their red masks. Pierrette went down the winding staircase with a light step, Gibiser behind her and Fridolin following in the rear. In the anteroom below Gibiser opened a door leading to the inner rooms and said to Pierrette: "Go to bed at once, you depraved creature. I'll talk to you as soon as I've settled with those two upstairs."

She stood in the doorway, white and delicate, and with a glance at Fridolin, sadly shook her head. He noticed with surprise, in a large wall-mirror to the right, a haggard pilgrim who seemed to be himself. At the same time he knew very well that it could be no other.

The girl disappeared and the old costumer locked the door behind her. Then he opened the entrance door and hurried Fridolin out into the hallway.

"Well," said Fridolin, "how much do I owe you?"

"Never mind, sir, you can pay when you return the things. I'll trust you."

Fridolin, however, refused to move. "Swear that you won't hurt that poor child," he said.

"What business is it of yours?"

"I heard you, a minute ago, say that the girl was insane—and just now you called her a depraved creature. That sounds pretty contradictory."

"Well," replied Gibiser theatrically, "aren't insanity and depravity the same in the eyes of God?"

Fridolin shuddered with disgust.

"Whatever it is," he remarked, "there are ways and means of attending to it. I am a doctor. We'll have another talk about this tomorrow."

Gibiser laughed mockingly without uttering a sound. A light flared up in the hallway, and the door between them was closed and immediately bolted. Fridolin took off the hat, cassock and mask while going downstairs, carrying the bundle under his arm. The caretaker opened the outer door and Fridolin saw the mourning-coach standing opposite with the motionless driver on the box. Nachtigall was just on the point of leaving the café, and seemed somewhat taken aback at seeing Fridolin at hand so promptly.

"Then you did manage to get a costume?"

"You can see for yourself. What's the password?"

"You insist on knowing it?"

"Absolutely."

"Well then—it's Denmark."

"Are you mad, Nachtigall?"

"Why mad?"

"Oh, never mind—I was at the seashore in Denmark this summer. Get back into your carriage—but not too fast, so that I'll have time to take a cab over on the other side."

Nachtigall nodded and leisurely lighted a cigarette. Fridolin quickly crossed the street, hailed a cab in an offhand way, as though he were playing a joke, and told the driver to follow the mourning-coach which was just starting in front of them.

They crossed Alser Strasse, and drove on through dim, deserted side-streets under a railroad viaduct toward the suburbs.

Fridolin was afraid that the driver might lose sight of the carriage, but whenever he put his head out of the open window, into the abnormally warm air, he always saw it. It was a moderate distance ahead of them, and the coachman with his high, black silk hat sat motionless on the box. This business may end badly, thought Fridolin. At the same time he remembered the fragrance of roses and powder that had arisen from Pierrette's breasts. What strange story is behind all that? He wondered. I shouldn't have left—perhaps it was even a great mistake—I wonder where I am now.

The road wound slowly uphill between modest villas. Fridolin thought that he now had his bearings. He had sometimes come this way on walks, years ago. It must be the *Galitzinberg* that he was going up. Down to his left he could see the city indistinct in the mist, but glimmering with a thousand lights. He heard the rumbling of wheels behind him and looked out of the window back of him. There were two carriages following his. He was glad of that, for now the driver of the mourning-coach would certainly not be suspicious of him.

With a violent jolt, the cab turned into a side street and went down into something like a ravine, between iron fences, stone walls and terraces. Fridolin realized that it was high time to put on his costume. He took off his fur coat and slipped into the cassock, just as he slipped into the sleeves of his white linen coat every morning in his ward at the hospital. He was relieved to think that, if everything went well, it would be only a few hours before he would be back again by the beds of his patients, ready to give aid.

His cab stopped. What if I don't get out at all, Fridolin thought, and go back at once? But go where? To little Pierrette? To the girl in Buchfeld Strasse? Or to Marianne, the daughter of the deceased? Or perhaps home? He shuddered slightly and decided he'd rather go anywhere than home. Was it because it was farthest to go? No, I can't turn back, he thought. I must go through with this, even if it means death. And he laughed at himself, using such a big word but without feeling very cheerful about it.

A garden gate stood wide open. The mourning-coach drove on deeper into the ravine, or into the darkness that seemed like one. Nachtigall must, therefore, have got out. Fridolin quickly sprang out of the cab and told the driver to wait for him up at the turn, no matter how late he might be. To make sure of him, he paid him well in advance and promised him a large sum for the return trip. The other carriages drove up and Fridolin saw the veiled figure of a woman step out of the first. Then he turned into the garden and put on his mask. A narrow path, lighted up by a lamp from the house, led to the entrance.

Doors opened before him, and he found himself in a narrow, white vestibule. He could hear an organ playing, and two servants in dark livery, their faces covered by gray masks, stood on each side of him.

Two voices whispered in unison: "Password?" He replied: "Denmark." One of them took his fur coat and disappeared with it into an adjoining room, while the other opened a door. Fridolin entered a dimly lighted room with high ceilings, hung on all sides with black silk. Sixteen to twenty people masked and dressed as monks and nuns were walking up and down. The gently swelling strains of Italian church music came from above. A small group, composed of three nuns and two monks, stood in a corner of the room. They watched him for a second, but turned away again at once, almost deliberately. Fridolin, noticing that he was the only one who wore a hat, took his off and walked up and down as nonchalantly as possible. A monk brushed against him and nodded a greeting, but from behind the mask Fridolin encountered a searching and penetrating glance. A strange, heavy perfume, as of Southern gardens, scented the room. Again an arm brushed against him, but this time it was that of a nun. Like all the others she had a black veil over her face, head and neck, a blood-red mouth glowed under the black laces of the mask. Where am I? Thought Fridolin. Among lunatics? Or conspirators? Is this a meeting of some religious sect? Can it be that Nachtigall was ordered or paid to bring along some stranger to be the target of their jokes? But everything seemed too serious, too intense, too uncanny for a masquerade prank. A woman's voice joined the strains of the organ and an Old Italian sacred aria resounded through the room. They all stood still and listened and Fridolin surrendered himself for a moment to the wondrously swelling melody. A soft voice suddenly whispered from behind: "Don't turn around. There's still a chance for you to get away. You don't belong here. If it's discovered it will go hard with you."

Fridolin gave a frightened start. For a second he thought of leaving, but his curiosity, the allurement and, above all, his pride, were stronger than any of his misgivings. Now that I've gone this far, he thought, I don't care what happens. And he shook his head negatively without turning around.

The voice behind him whispered: "I should feel very sorry for you." He turned and looked at her. He saw the blood-red mouth glimmering under the lace. Dark eyes were fixed on him. "I shall stay," he said in a heroic voice which he hardly recognized as his own, and he looked away again. The song was now ringing through the room; the organ had a new sound which was anything but sacred. It was worldly, voluptuous, and pealing. Looking around Fridolin saw that all the nuns had disappeared and that only the monks were left. The voice had meanwhile also changed. It rose by way of an artistically executed trill from its low and serious pitch to a high and jubilant tone. In place of the organ a piano had suddenly chimed in with its worldly and brazen tunes. Fridolin at once recognized Nachtigall's wild and inflammatory touch. The woman's voice which had been so reverent a moment before had vanished with a last wild, voluptuous outburst through the ceiling, as it were, into infinity. Doors opened to the right and left On one side Fridolin recognized the indistinct outlines of Nachtigall's figure; the room opposite was radiant with a blaze of light. All the women were standing there motionless. They wore dark veils over their heads, faces and necks and black masks over their eyes, but otherwise they were completely naked. Fridolin's eyes wandered eagerly from voluptuous to slender bodies, from delicate figures to those luxuriously developed. He realized that each of these women would forever be a mystery, and that the enigma of their large eyes peering at him from beneath the black masks would remain unsolved. The delight of beholding was changed to an almost unbearable agony of desire. And the others seemed to experience a similar sensation. The first gasps of rapture had changed to sighs that held a note very near anguish. A cry broke out somewhere. Suddenly all of them, as though pursued, rushed from the darkened room to the women, who received them with wild and wicked laughter. The men were no longer in cassocks, but dressed as cavaliers, in white, yellow, blue and red. Fridolin was the only one in monk's dress. Somewhat nervously he slunk into the farthest corner, where he was near Nachtigall whose back was turned to him. Nachtigall had a bandage over his eyes, but Fridolin thought he could see him peering underneath the bandage into the tall mirror opposite. In it the cavaliers with their gay-colored costumes were reflected, dancing with their naked partners.

A woman came up suddenly behind Fridolin and whispered— for no one spoke aloud, as if the voices, too, were to remain a secret—: "What is the matter? Why don't you dance?"

Fridolin, seeing two noblemen watch fixedly from another corner, suspected that this woman with the boyish and slender figure, was sent to put him to the test. In spite of it he meant to dance with her, but at that moment another woman left her partner and walked quickly up to him. He knew at once that it was the same one who had already warned him. She pretended that she had just seen him and whispered, in a voice loud enough to be heard in the other corner: "Returned at last!" Laughingly, she continued: "All your efforts are useless. I know you." Then turning to the woman with the boyish figure, she said: "Let me have him for just two minutes, then he shall be yours again until morning, if you wish." In a softer voice she added: "It is really he." The other replied in astonishment: "Really?" and with a light step went to join the cavaliers in the corner.

Alone with Fridolin, the woman cautioned him, "Don't ask questions, and don't be surprised at anything. I tried to lead them astray, but you can't continue to deceive them for long. Go, before it is too late—and it may be too late at almost any moment—and be careful that no one follows you. No one must know who you are. There would be no more peace and quiet for you. Go!"

"Will I see you again?"

"It's impossible."

"Then I shall stay."

"My life, at most, is at stake," he said, "and I'm ready at this moment to give it for you." He took her hands and tried to draw her to him.

She whispered again, almost despairingly: "Go!"

He laughed, and he heard himself laughing as in a dream. "But I know what I'm doing. You are not all here just to make us mad by looking at you. You are doing this to unnerve me still more."

"It will soon be too late. You must go!"

But he wouldn't listen to her. "Do you mean to say that there are no rooms here for the convenience of congenial couples? Will all these people leave with just a courteous 'goodbye'? They don't look like it."

He pointed to the dancers, glowing white bodies closely pressed against the blue, red and yellow silk of their partners, circling, in the brilliant, mirrored room adjoining, to the wild tunes of the piano. It seemed to him that no longer was any attention paid to him and the woman beside him. They stood alone in the semi-dark middle room.

"You are hoping in vain," she whispered. "There are no such rooms here. This is your last opportunity to leave."

"Come with me!"

She shook her head violently, despairingly.

He laughed again, not recognizing his laughter. "You're making game of me. Did all these men and women come here merely to fan the flames of their desire and then depart? Who can forbid you to come away with me if you choose?"

She took a deep breath and drooped her head.

"Oh, now I understand," he said. "That's the punishment you impose on those who come here uninvited. You couldn't have invented a more cruel one. Please let me off and forgive me. Impose some other penalty, anything but that I must leave you."

"You are mad. I can't go with you, let alone anyone else. Whomever I went with would forfeit his life and mine."

Fridolin felt intoxicated, not only with her, her fragrant body and her red-glowing mouth—not only with the atmosphere of this room and the voluptuous mysteries that surrounded him—he was intoxicated, his thirst unsatisfied, with all the experiences of the night, none of which had come to a satisfactory conclusion. He was intoxicated with himself, with his boldness, the change he felt in himself, and he touched the veil which was wound about her head, as though he intended to remove it.

She seized his hands. "One night during the dance here one of the men took it into his head to tear the veil from one of us. They ripped the mask from his face and drove him out with whips."

"And—she?"

"Did you read of a beautiful young girl, only a few weeks ago, who took poison the day before her wedding?"

He remembered the incident, even the name, and mentioned it. "Wasn't it a girl of the nobility who was engaged to marry an Italian Prince?"

She nodded.

One of the cavaliers, the most distinguished looking of them all and the only one dressed in white, suddenly stopped before them. With a slight bow, courteous but imperative, he asked the woman with whom Fridolin was talking to dance with him. She seemed to hesitate a moment, but he put his arm around her waist and they drifted away to join the other couples in the adjoining room.

A sudden feeling of solitude made Fridolin shiver as if with cold. He looked about him. Nobody seemed to be paying any attention to him. This was perhaps his last chance to leave with impunity. He didn't know, however, why it was that he remained spellbound in his corner where he now felt sure that he was not observed. It might be his aversion to an inglorious and perhaps ridiculous retreat, or the excruciating ungratified desire for the beautiful woman whose fragrance was still in his nostrils. Or he may have stayed because he vaguely hoped that all that had happened so far was intended as a test of his courage and that this magnificent woman would be his reward. It was clear at any rate that the strain was too great to be endured, and that, no matter what the danger, he would have to end it. It could hardly cost him his life, no matter what he decided. He might be among fools, or libertines, but certainly not among rascals or criminals. The thought occurred to him to acknowledge himself as an intruder and to place himself at their disposal in chivalrous fashion. This night could only conclude in such a manner,—with a harmonious finale, as it were—if it were to mean more than a wild, shadow-like succession of gloomy and lascivious adventures, all without an end. So, taking a deep breath, he prepared to carry out his plan.

At this moment, however, a voice whispered beside him: "Password!" A cavalier in black had stepped up to him unseen. As Fridolin didn't reply, he repeated his question. "Denmark," said Fridolin.

"That's right, sir, that's the password for admittance, but what's the password of the house, may I ask?" Fridolin was silent.

"Won't you be kind enough to tell me the password of the house?" It sounded like a sharp threat.

Fridolin shrugged his shoulders. The other walked to the middle of the room and raised his hand. The piano ceased playing and the dance stopped. Two other cavaliers, one in yellow, the other in red, stepped up. "The password, sir," they said simultaneously.

"I have forgotten it," replied Fridolin with a vacant smile but feeling quite calm.

"That's unfortunate," said the gentleman in yellow, "for here it doesn't matter whether you have forgotten it or if you never knew it."

The other men flocked in and the doors on both sides were closed. Fridolin stood alone in the garb of a monk in the midst of the gay-colored cavaliers.

ARTHUR SCHNITZLER

"Take off your mask!" several of them demanded. Fridolin held out his arm to protect himself. It seemed a thousand times worse to be the only one unmasked amongst so many that were, than to stand suddenly naked amongst people who were dressed. He replied firmly: "If my appearance here has offended any of the gentlemen present, I am ready to give satisfaction in the usual manner, but I shall take off my mask only if all of you will do the same."

"It's not a question of satisfaction," said the cavalier in red, who until now had not spoken, "but one of expiation."

"Take off your mask!" commanded another in a high-pitched, insolent voice which reminded Fridolin of an officer giving orders, "and we'll tell you to your face what's in store for you."

"I shall not take it off," said Fridolin in an even sharper tone, "and woe to him who dares to touch me."

A hand suddenly reached out, as if to tear off the mask, when a door suddenly opened and one of the women—Fridolin did not doubt which one it was—stood there, dressed as a nun, as he had first seen her. The others could be seen behind her in the brilliantly lighted room, naked, with veiled faces, crowding together in a terrified group. The door at once closed again.

"Leave him alone," said the nun. "I am ready to redeem him."

There was a short, deep silence, as though something monstrous had happened. The cavalier in black who had first demanded the password from Fridolin turned to the nun, saying: "You know what you are taking upon yourself in doing this."

"I know."

There was a general sigh of relief from those present.

"You are free," said the cavalier to Fridolin. "Leave this house at once and be careful not to inquire further into what you have seen here. If you attempt to put anyone on our trail, whether you succeed or not—you will be doomed."

Fridolin stood motionless. "How is this woman—to redeem me?" he asked.

There was no answer. Hands pointed to the door indicated that he must go.

Fridolin shook his head. "Impose what punishment you wish, gentlemen, I won't let this woman pay for me."

"You would be unable, in any case, to change her lot," the cavalier in black said very gently. "When a promise has been made here there is no turning back."

The nun slowly nodded, as if to confirm the statement. "Go!" she said to Fridolin.

"No," replied the latter, elevating his voice. "Life means nothing to me if I must leave here without you. I shall not ask who you are or where you come from. What difference can it make to you, gentlemen, whether or not you keep up this carnival comedy, though it may aim at a serious conclusion. Whoever you may be, you surely lead other lives. I won't play a part, here or elsewhere, and if I have been forced to do so up to now, I shall give it up. I feel that a fate has overtaken me which has nothing to do with this foolery. I will tell you my name, take off my mask and be responsible for the consequences."

"Don't do it," exclaimed the nun, "you would only ruin yourself without saving me. Go!" Then she turned to the others, saying: "Here I am, take me—all of you!" The dark costume dropped from her, as if by magic. She stood there in the radiance of her white body; reached for the veil which was wrapped about her head, face and neck and unwound it with a wonderful circular motion. It sank to the floor, dark hair fell in great profusion over her shoulders, breasts and hips—but before Fridolin could even glance at her face, he was seized by irresistible arms, and pushed to the door. A moment later he found himself in the anteroom, the door closed behind him. A masked servant brought him his fur coat and helped him put it on. The main door opened automatically, and as if driven by some invisible force, he hurried out. As he stood on the street the light behind disappeared. The house stood there in silence with closed windows from which not a glimmer issued. I must remember everything clearly, was his main thought; I must find the house again—the rest will follow as a matter of course.

Darkness surrounded him. The dull reddish glow of a street lamp was visible a slight distance above where the cab was to wait for him. The mourning-coach drove up from the street below, as though he had called it. A servant opened the door.

"I have my own cab," said Fridolin. When the servant shook his head, Fridolin continued: "If it has already gone, I'll walk back to the city."

The man replied with a wave of his hand which was anything but servant-like, so that objection was out of the question. The ridiculously high silk hat of the coachman towered up into the night. The wind was blowing a gale; violet clouds raced across the sky. Fridolin felt that, after his previous experience, there was nothing for him to do but to get into the carriage. It started the moment he was inside.

He resolved, as soon as possible, to clear up the mystery of his adventure, no matter how dangerous it might be. His life, it seemed, would not have the slightest meaning anymore, if he did not succeed in finding the incomprehensible woman who at this very moment was paying for his safety. It was only too easy to guess the price. But why should she sacrifice herself for him? To sacrifice—? Was she the kind of woman to whom the things that were facing her, that she was now submitting to, could mean a sacrifice? If she attended these affairs—and since she seemed to understand the rules so well it could not be her first time—what difference could it make to her if she belonged to one of the cavaliers, or to all? Indeed, could she possibly be anything but a woman of easy virtue? Were any of them anything else? That's what they were, without a doubt, even if all of them led another, more normal life, so to speak, besides this one of promiscuity. Perhaps everything he had just gone through had been only an outrageous joke. A joke planned, prepared and even rehearsed for such an occasion when some bold outsider should be caught intruding?

And yet, as he thought of the woman who had warned him from the very beginning, who was now ready to pay for him—he remembered something in her voice, her bearing, in the royal nobility of her nude body which could not possibly have been false. Or was it possible that only his sudden appearance had caused her to change? After everything that had happened, such a supposition did not seem impossible. There was no conceit in this idea. There may be hours or nights, he thought, in which some strange, irresistible charm emanates from men who under normal circumstances have no special power over the other sex.

The carriage continued uphill. If all were well, he should have turned into the main street long ago. What were they going to do with him? Where was the carriage taking him? Was the comedy to be continued elsewhere? And what would the continuation be? A solution of the mystery and a happy reunion at someother place. Would he be rewarded for passing the test so creditably and made a member of the secret society? Was he to have unchallenged possession of the lovely nun? The windows of the carriage were closed and Fridolin tried to look out—but they were opaque. He attempted to open them, first on one side, then on the other, but it was impossible. The glass partition between him and the coachman's box was just as thick and just as firmly closed. He knocked on the glass, he called, he shouted, but the carriage went on. He tried to open both the doors, but they wouldn't budge. His renewed calling was drowned by the rattling of the wheels and the roaring of the wind. The carriage began to jolt, going down-hill, faster and faster. Fridolin, uneasy and alarmed, was on the point of smashing one of the blind windows, when the carriage suddenly stopped. Both doors opened together, as if by some mechanism, and as though Fridolin had been ironically given the choice between one side or the other. He jumped out, the doors closed with a bang—and without the coachman paying the slightest attention to him, the carriage drove away across the open field into the darkness of the night.

The sky was overcast, clouds raced across it, and the wind whistled. Fridolin stood in the snow which shed a faint light round about. He was alone, his open fur coat over his monk's costume, the pilgrim's hat on his head; and an uncanny feeling overcame him. The main street was a slight distance away, where a row of dimly-flickering street lamps indicated the direction of the city. However, he ran straight down across the sloping, snow-covered field, which shortened the way, so as to get among people as quickly as possible. His feet soaked, he came into a narrow, almost unlighted street, and at first walked along between high board fences which groaned in the wind. Turning the next corner,

　　　　　　　　　　　ARTHUR SCHNITZLER

he reached a somewhat wider street, where scattered little houses alternated with empty building lots. Somewhere a tower clock struck three.

Someone was coming towards him. The person wore a short jacket, he had his hands in his trouser pockets, his head was down between his shoulders, and his hat was pulled over his forehead. Fridolin got ready for an attack, but the tramp unexpectedly turned and ran. What does that mean? he asked himself. Then he decided that he must present a very uncanny appearance, took off the pilgrim's hat and buttoned his coat, underneath which the monk's gown was flapping around his ankles. Again he turned a corner into a suburban main street. A man in peasant's dress walked past and spoke to him, thinking him a priest. The light of a street lamp fell upon a sign on a corner house. *Liebhartstal*— then he wasn't very far from the house which he had left less than an hour before. For a second he felt tempted to retrace his steps and to wait in the vicinity for further developments. But he gave up the idea when he realized that he would only expose himself to grave danger without solving the mystery. As he imagined what was probably taking place in the villa at this very moment he was filled with wrath, despair, shame and fear. This state of mind was so unbearable that it almost made him sorry the tramp had not attacked him; in fact, he almost regretted that he wasn't lying against the fence in the deserted street with a knife-gash in his side. That, at least, might have given some significance to this senseless night with its childish adventures, all of which had been so ruthlessly cut short. It seemed positively ridiculous to return home, as he now intended doing. But nothing was lost as yet. There was another day ahead, and he swore that he would not rest until he had found again the beautiful woman whose dazzling nakedness had so intoxicated him. It was only now that he thought of Albertina, but with a feeling that she, too, would first have to be won. He could not, must not, be reunited with her until he had deceived her with all the other women of the night. With the naked woman, with Pierrette, with Marianne, with Mizzi in the narrow street. And shouldn't he also try to find the insolent student who had bumped into him, so that he might challenge him to a duel with sabres or, better still, with pistols? What did someone else's life, what did his own, matter to him? Is one always to stake one's life just from a sense of duty or self-sacrifice, and never because of a whim or a passion, or simply to match oneself against Fate?

Again the thought came to him that even now the germ of a fatal disease might be in his body. Wouldn't it be silly to die just because a child with diphtheria had coughed in his face? Perhaps he was already ill. Wasn't he feverish? Perhaps at this moment he was lying at home in bed—and everything he thought he had experienced was merely delirium?

Fridolin opened his eyes as wide as possible, passed his hand over his forehead and cheeks and felt his pulse. It scarcely beat faster. Everything was all right. He was completely awake.

He continued along the street, towards the city. A few market-wagons rumbled by, and now and then he met poorly dressed people whose day was just beginning. Behind the window of a coffeehouse, at a table over which a gas-flame flickered, sat a fat man with a scarf around his neck, his head on his hands, fast asleep. The houses were still enveloped in darkness, though here and there a few windows were lighted and Fridolin thought he could feel the people gradually awaking. It seemed that he could see them stretching themselves in their beds and preparing for their pitiful and strenuous day. A new day faced him, too, but for him it wasn't pitiful and dull. And with a strange, happy beating of his heart, he realized that in a few hours he would be walking around between the beds of his patients in his white hospital coat. A one-horse cab stood at the next corner, the coachman asleep on the box. Fridolin awakened him, gave his address and got in.

V

It was four o'clock in the morning when Fridolin walked up the steps of his home. Before doing anything else he went into his office and carefully locked the masquerade costume in a closet. As he wished not to wake Albertina, he took off his shoes and clothes before going into the bedroom, and very cautiously turned on the light on the little table beside his bed. Albertina was lying there quietly, with her arms folded under her head. Her lips were half-open, and painful shadows surrounded them. It was a face that Fridolin did not know. He bent down over her, and at once her forehead became lined with furrows, as though someone had touched it, and her features seemed strangely distorted. Suddenly, still in her sleep, she laughed so shrilly that he became frightened. Involuntarily he called her name. She laughed again, as if in answer, in a strange, almost uncanny manner. Fridolin called her in a louder voice, and she opened her eyes, slowly and with difficulty. She stared at him, as though she did not recognize him.

"Albertina!" he cried for the third time. As she gained consciousness, an expression of fear, even of terror came into her eyes. Half awake, and seemingly in despair, she raised her arms.

"What's the matter?" asked Fridolin with bated breath. As she still stared at him, terrified, he added, to reassure her: "It is I, Albertina." She breathed deeply, tried to smile, dropped her arms on the bed cover and said, in a far away voice: "Is it morning yet?"

"It will be very soon," replied Fridolin, "it's past four o'clock. I've just come home." She was silent and he continued: "The Councilor is dead. He was dying when I arrived, and naturally I couldn't—leave immediately."

She nodded, but hardly seemed to have heard or understood him. She stared into space, as though she could see through him. He felt that she must know of his recent experiences—and at the same time the idea seemed ridiculous. He bent down and touched her forehead. She shuddered slightly.

"What's the matter?" he asked again.

She shook her head slowly and he passed his hand gently over her hair. "Albertina, what's the matter?"

"I've been dreaming," she said distantly.

"What have you been dreaming?" he asked mildly.

"Oh, so much, I can't quite remember."

"Perhaps if you try?"

"It was all so confused—and I'm tired. You must be tired, too."

"Not in the least. I don't think I shall go to bed at all. You know, when I come home so late—it would really be best to sit right down to my desk—it's just in such morning hours—" He interrupted himself. "Wouldn't it be better if you told me your dream?" He smiled a little unnaturally.

She replied: "You really ought to lie down and take a little rest."

He hesitated a moment, then he did as she suggested and stretched himself beside her, though he was careful not to touch her. There shall be a sword between us, he thought, remembering a remark he had once made, half joking, on a similar occasion. They lay there silently with open eyes, and they felt both their proximity and the distance that separated them. After a while he raised his head on his arm and looked at her for a long time, as though he could see much more than just the outlines of her face.

"Your dream!" he hinted, once more. She must just have been waiting for him to speak. She held out her hand to him, he took it and, more absentmindedly than tenderly, clasped his hand about her slender fingers, as he had often done before. She began: "Do you still remember the room in the little villa on Lake Wörther, where I lived with Mother and Father the summer we became engaged?"

He nodded.

"Well, it was there the dream began. I was entering this house, like an actress stepping onto the stage—I don't know where I came from. My parents seemed to have gone on a journey and left me alone. That surprised me, for our wedding was the next day. But my wedding dress hadn't yet arrived. I thought I might be mistaken, and I opened the wardrobe to look. Instead of the wedding dress a great many other clothes, like fancy dress costumes, were hanging there, opera-like, gorgeous, Oriental. Which shall I wear for the wedding? I thought. Then the wardrobe was suddenly closed again, or it disappeared, I don't remember. The room was brightly lighted, but outside the window it was pitch black. . . Suddenly you were standing out there. Galley slaves had rowed you to the house. I had just seen them disappearing in the darkness. You were dressed in marvelous gold and silver clothes, and had a dagger in a silver sheath hanging by your side. You lifted me down from the window. I, too, was gorgeously dressed, like a princess. We stood outside in the twilight, and a fine gray mist reached up to our ankles. The countryside was perfectly familiar to us: there was the lake, the mountain rose above us, and I could even see the villas which stood there like little toy houses. We were floating, no, flying, along above the mist, and I thought: so this is our honeymoon trip. Soon, however, we stopped flying and were walking along a forest path, the one leading to Elizabeth Heights. Suddenly, we came into a sort of clearing in the mountains enclosed on three sides by the forest, while a steep wall of rock towered up in the back. The sky was blue and starry, with an expanse far greater than it ever has in reality; it was the ceiling of our bridal-chamber. You took me into your arms and loved me very much."

"I hope you loved me, too," remarked Fridolin with an invisible, malicious smile.

"Even more than you did me," replied Albertina seriously, "but, how can I explain it—in spite of the intensity of our happiness our love was also sad, as if filled with some presentiment of sorrow. Suddenly, it was morning. The meadow was light and covered with flowers, the forest glistened with dew, and over the rocky wall the sun sent down quivering rays of light. It was now time to return to the world and go among people. But something terrible happened: our clothes were gone. I was seized with unheard of terror and a shame so burning that it almost consumed me. At the same time I was angry with you, as though you were to blame for the misfortune. This sensation of terror, shame and anger was much more intense than anything I had ever felt when awake. Conscious of your guilt, you rushed away naked, to go and get clothes for us. When you had gone I was very gay. I neither felt sorry for you, nor worried about you. Delighted to be alone, I ran happily about in the meadow singing a tune we had heard at some dance. My voice had a wonderful ring and I wished that they could hear me down in the city, which I couldn't see but which nevertheless existed. It was far below me and was surrounded by a high wall, a very fantastic city which I can't describe. It was not Oriental and not exactly Old-German, and yet it seemed to be first one, and then the other. At any rate, it was a city buried a long time ago and forever. Suddenly I was lying in the meadow, stretched out in the sunlight—far more beautiful than I ever was in reality, and while I lay there, a young man wearing a light-colored fashionable suit of clothes walked out of the woods. I now realize that he looked like the Dane whom I mentioned yesterday. He walked up and spoke to me courteously as he passed, but otherwise paid no particular attention to me. He went straight to the wall of rock and looked it over carefully, as though considering how to master it. At the same time I could see you hurrying from house to house, from shop to shop in the buried city, now walking underneath arbors, then passing through a sort of Turkish bazaar. You were buying the most beautiful things you could find for me: clothes, linen, shoes, and jewelry. And then you put these things into a little handbag of yellow leather that held them all. You were being followed by a crowd of people whom I could not see, but I heard the sound of their threatening shouts. The Dane, who had stopped before the wall of rock a little while before, now reappeared from the woods—and apparently in the meantime he had encircled the whole globe. He looked different, but he was the same, nevertheless. He stopped before the wall of rock, vanished and came out of the woods again, appearing and disappearing two, or three, or a hundred times. It was always the same man and yet always different. He spoke to me everytime he passed, and finally stopped in front of me and looked at me searchingly. I laughed seductively as I have never laughed in my life, and he held out his arms to me. I wished to escape but it was useless—and he sank down beside me on the meadow."

ARTHUR SCHNITZLER

She was silent. Fridolin's throat was parched. In the darkness of the room he could see she had concealed her face in her hands.

"A strange dream," he said, "but surely that isn't the end?" When she said "no," he asked: "Then why don't you continue?"

"It's not easy," she began again. "Such things are difficult to express in words. Well, to go on—I seemed to live through countless days and nights; there was neither time nor space. I was no longer in the clearing, enclosed by the woods and rock. I was on a flower-covered plain, that stretched into infinite distance and, finally, into the horizon in all directions. And for a long time I had not been alone with this one man on the meadow. Whether there were three, .or ten, or a thousand other couples I don't know. Whether I noticed them or not, whether I was united only with that particular man or also with others, I can't say. Just as that earlier feeling of terror and shame went beyond anything I have ever felt in the waking state, so nothing in our conscious existence can be compared with the feeling of release, of freedom, of happiness, which I now experienced. Yet I didn't for one moment forget you. In fact, I saw that you had been seized— by soldiers, I think—and there were also priests among them. Somebody, a gigantic person, tied your hands, and I knew that you were to be executed. I knew it, without feeling any sympathy for you, and without shuddering. I felt it, but as though I were far removed from you. They led you into a yard, a sort of castle-yard, and you stood there, naked, with your hands tied behind your back. Just as I saw you, though I was far away, you could also see me and the man who was holding me in his arms. All the other couples, too, were visible in this infinite sea of nakedness which foamed about me, and of which my companion and I were only a wave, so to speak. Then, while you were standing in the castle-yard, a young woman, with a diadem on her head and wearing a purple cloak, appeared at a high arched window between red curtains. It was the queen of the country, and she looked down at you with a stern, questioning look. You were standing alone. All the others stood aside, pressed against the wall, and I heard them whispering and muttering in a malicious and threatening manner. Then the queen bent down over the railing. Silence reigned, and she signaled to you, commanding you to come up to her, and I knew that she had decided to pardon you. But you either didn't notice her, or else you didn't want to. Suddenly you were standing opposite her, with your hands still tied. You were wrapped in a black cloak, and you were not in a room, but in the open, somehow, floating, as it were. She held a piece of parchment in her hand, your death sentence, which stated your crime and the reasons for your conviction. She asked you—I couldn't hear the words, but I knew it was so—whether you were willing to be her lover, for in that case the death-penalty would be remitted. You shook your head, refusing. I wasn't surprised, for it seemed natural and inevitable that you should be faithful to me, under all circumstances. The queen shrugged her shoulders, waved her hand, and suddenly you were in a subterranean cellar, and whips were whizzing down upon you, although I couldn't see the people who were swinging them. Blood flowed down you in streams. I saw it without feeling cruel, or even surprised. The queen now moved towards you, her loose hair flowing about her naked body, and held out her diadem to you with both hands. I realized that she was the girl at the seashore in Denmark, the one you had once seen nude, in the morning, on the ledge of a bathing-hut. She didn't say a word, but she was clearly there to learn if you would be her husband and the ruler of the land. When you refused again, she suddenly disappeared. At the same time I saw them erecting a cross for you—not down in the castle- yard, but on the meadow, where I was resting with my lover among all the other couples. I saw you walking alone through ancient streets without a guard, but I knew that your course was marked out for you and that it was impossible for you to turn aside. Next, you were coming up the forest path, where I anxiously awaited you, but I did not feel any sympathy for you, though your body was covered with the weals which had stopped bleeding. You went higher and higher, the path widened, the forest receded on both sides, and you stood at the edge of the meadow at an enormous, incomprehensible distance. Your eyes smiled at me as if to show that you had fulfilled my wish and had brought me everything I needed: clothing and shoes and jewels. But I thought your actions senseless beyond description and I wanted to make fun of you, to laugh in your face—because you had refused the queen's hand out of faithfulness to me. And because you had been tortured and now came tottering up here to a horrible death. As I ran to meet you, you came near more and more quickly. We were floating in the air, and then I lost sight of you; and I realized we had flown past each other. I hoped that you would, at least, hear my laughter when they were nailing you to the cross.—And so I laughed, as shrill and loud as I could—that was the laugh, Fridolin, that you heard—when I awoke."

Neither of them spoke or moved. Any remark at this moment would have seemed futile. The further her story progressed, the more ridiculous and insignificant did his own experiences become, at least up to date. He swore to himself that he would resume and conclude all of them. He would then faithfully report them and so take vengeance on this woman who had revealed herself as faithless, cruel and treacherous, and whom he now believed he hated more than he had ever loved her.

He realized that he was still clasping her fingers. Ready as he was to hate her, his feeling of tenderness for these slender, cool fingers was unchanged except that it was more acute. Involuntarily, in fact against his will, he gently pressed his lips on this familiar hand before he let it go.

Albertina still kept her eyes closed and Fridolin thought he could see a happy, innocent smile playing about her mouth. He felt an incomprehensible desire to bend over her and kiss her pale forehead. But he checked himself. He realized that it was only the natural fatigue of the last few hours which disguised itself as tenderness in the familiarity of their mutual room.

But whatever his present state of mind—whatever decisions he might reach in the next few hours, the urgent demand of the moment was for sleep and forgetfulness. He had been able to sleep long and dreamlessly the night following the death of his mother, so why not now? He stretched himself out beside his wife who seemed already asleep. A sword between us, he thought, we are lying here like mortal enemies. But it was only an illusion.

VI

At seven o'clock Fridolin was awakened by the maid gently knocking on the door, and he cast a quick glance at Albertina. Sometimes this knocking awakened her too. But today she was sleeping soundly; too soundly Fridolin thought. He dressed himself quickly, intending to see his little daughter before leaving. The child lay quietly in her white bed, her hands clenched into little fists, as children do in sleep, and he kissed her on her forehead. Tiptoeing to the door of the bedroom he found Albertina still sleeping soundly; then he went out. The cassock and pilgrim's hat were safely concealed in his black doctor's bag. He had drawn up a program for the day with great care, indeed, even a bit pedantically. First of all he had to see a young attorney in the neighborhood who was seriously ill. Fridolin made a careful examination and found his condition somewhat improved. He expressed his satisfaction with sincere joy and ordered an old prescription to be refilled. Then he went to the house in the basement of which Nachtigall had played the piano the night before. The place was still closed, but the girl at the counter in the café above said that Nachtigall lived in a small hotel in *Leopoldstadt*. He took a cab and arrived there a quarter of an hour later. It was a very shabby place, smelling of unaired beds, rancid lard and chicory. A tough looking concierge, with sly, inflamed eyes, wishing to keep on good terms with the police, willingly gave information. Herr Nachtigall had arrived in a cab at five o'clock in the morning, accompanied by two men who had disguised their faces, perhaps intentionally so, with scarfs which they wore wrapped about their heads and necks. While Nachtigall was in his room, the two men had paid his bill for the last four weeks. When he didn't appear after half an hour, one of them had gone up to fetch him, whereupon they all three took a cab to North Station. Nachtigall had seemed highly excited, in fact—well, why not tell the whole truth to a man who gave one so much confidence—he had tried to slip a letter to the concierge, but the two men stopped that. Any letters for Herr Nachtigall—

so the men had explained—would be called for by a person properly authorized to do so. Fridolin took his leave. He was glad that he had his doctor's bag with him when he stepped out of the door, for anyone seeing him would not think that he was staying at the hotel, but would take him for some official person. There was nothing to be done about Nachtigall for the time being. They had been extremely cautious, probably with good reason.

At the costume shop, Herr Gibiser himself opened the door. "I'm bringing back the costume I hired," said Fridolin, "and would like to pay my bill." The proprietor mentioned a moderate sum, took the money and made an entry in a large ledger. He looked up, evidently surprised, when Fridolin made no move to leave.

"I would also like," said Fridolin in the tone of a police magistrate, "to have a word with you about your daughter."

There was a peculiar expression about the nostrils of Herr Gibiser—it was difficult to say whether it was displeasure, scorn or annoyance.

"What did you say?" he asked in a perfectly indefinite voice.

"Yesterday you said," remarked Fridolin, one hand with outstretched fingers resting on the desk, "that your daughter was not quite normal mentally. The situation in which we discovered her actually indicates some such thing. And since I took part in it, or was at least a spectator, I would very much like to advise you to consult a doctor."

Gibiser surveyed Fridolin insolently, twirling an unnaturally long pen-holder in his hand.

"And I suppose the doctor himself would like to take charge of the treatment?

"Please don't misunderstand me," replied Fridolin in a sharp voice.

At this moment the door which led to the inner rooms was opened, and a young man with an open top coat over his evening clothes stepped out. Fridolin decided it could be none other than one of the vehmic judges of the night before. He undoubtedly came from Pierrette's room. He seemed taken aback when he caught sight of Fridolin, but he regained his composure at once.

He waved his hand to Gibiser, lighted a cigarette with a match from the desk, and left the apartment.

"Oh, that's how it is," remarked Fridolin with a contemptuous twitch of his mouth and a bitter taste on his tongue.

"What did you say?" asked Gibiser with perfect equanimity.

"So you have changed your mind about notifying the police," said Fridolin as his eyes wandered significantly from the entrance door to that of Pierrette.

"We have come to another agreement," remarked Gibiser coldly, and got up as though this were the end of an interview. He obligingly opened the door as Fridolin turned to go and said, without changing his expression: "If the doctor should want anything again. . . it needn't necessarily be a monk's costume."

Fridolin slammed the door behind him. So that is settled, he thought, as he hurried down the stairs with a feeling of annoyance which, even to him, seemed exaggerated. The first thing he did on arriving at the Polyclinic was to telephone home to inquire whether any patients had sent for him, if there was any mail, or any other news. The maid had scarcely answered him when Albertina herself came to the phone to answer Fridolin's call. She repeated everything the maid had already told him, and then said casually that she had just got up and was going to have breakfast with the child. "Give her a kiss for me," said Fridolin, "and I hope you enjoy your breakfast."

It had been pleasant to hear her voice but he quickly hung up the receiver. Although he had really wanted to know what she planned to do during the forenoon, what business was it of his? Down in the bottom of his heart he was through with her, no matter how their surface life continued. The blond nurse helped him to take off his coat and handed him his white linen one, smiling at him just as they all did, whether one paid attention to them or not.

A few minutes later he was in the ward. The physician in charge had suddenly sent word that he had to leave the city for a conference, and that the assistants should make the rounds without him. Fridolin felt almost happy as he walked from bed to bed, followed by the students, making examinations, writing prescriptions, and having professional conversations with the assistants and nurses. Various changes had taken place. The journeyman-locksmith, Karl Rödel, had died during the night and the autopsy was to take place at half past four in the afternoon. A bed had become vacant in the woman's ward, but was again occupied. The woman in bed seventeen had had to be transferred to the surgical division. Besides this, there was a lot of personal gossip. The appointment of a man for the ophthalmology division would be decided day after tomorrow. Hügelmann, at present professor at the University of Marburg, had the best chances, although four years ago he had been merely a second assistant to Stellwag. That's quick promotion, thought Fridolin. I'll never be considered for the headship of a department, if for no other reason than that I've never been a *Dozent*. It's too late. But why should it be? I really ought to begin again to do scientific work or take up more seriously some of the things that I have already started. My private practice would leave me ample time for it. He asked Doctor Fuchstaler if he would please take charge of the dispensary. He confessed to himself that he would rather have stayed there than drive out to *Galitzinberg*. And yet, he must. He felt obliged, not only for his own sake, to investigate this matter further, but there were all sorts of other things to be settled that day. He decided to ask Doctor Fuchstaler to take charge of the afternoon rounds, too, so as to be prepared for all emergencies. The young girl, over there, with suspected tuberculosis was smiling at him. It was the same one who had recently pressed her breasts so confidingly against his cheek when he examined her. Fridolin gave her a cold look and turned away with a frown. They are all alike, he thought bitterly, and Albertina is like the rest of them—if not the worst. I won't live with her any longer. Things can never be the same again. On the stairs he spoke to a colleague from the surgical division. Well, how was the woman who had been transferred during the night getting along? As far as he was concerned, he didn't really think it was necessary to operate. They would, of course, tell him the result of the histological examination?

"Why certainly, doctor."

He took a cab at the corner, consulting his notebook and pretending to the cabman that he was making up his mind where to go. "To *Ottakring*," he then said, "take the street going out to *Galitzinberg*. I'll tell you where to stop."

When he was in the cab he suddenly became terribly restless. In fact, he almost had a guilty conscience, because, during the last few hours, he had nearly forgotten the beautiful woman who had saved him. Would he now find the house? Well, that shouldn't be particularly difficult. The only question was what to do when he had found it. Notify the police? That might have disastrous consequences for the woman who had sacrificed herself for him, or had, at least, been ready to do so. Should he go to a private detective agency? He thought that would be in rather bad taste and not particularly dignified. But what else could he possibly do? He hadn't the time or the skill to make the necessary investigations. A secret club? Well, yes, it certainly was secret, though they seemed to know each other. Were they aristocrats, or perhaps even members of the court? He thought of certain archdukes who might easily be capable of such behavior. And what about the women? Probably they were recruited from brothels.

Well, that was not by any means certain, but at any rate, they seemed very attractive. But how about the woman who had sacrificed herself for him? Sacrificed? Why did he try, again and again, to make himself believe that it really was a sacrifice? It had been a joke, of course; the whole thing had been a joke and he ought to be grateful to have gotten out of the scrape so easily. Well, why not? He had preserved his dignity, and the cavaliers probably realized that he was nobody's fool. And she must have realized it also. Very likely she had cared more for him than for all those archdukes or whatever they were.

He got out at the end of *Liebhartstal*, where the road led sharply uphill, and took the precaution of sending the cab away. There were white clouds in the pale-blue sky and the sun shone with the warmth of spring. He looked back—there was nothing suspicious in sight, no cab, no pedestrian. He walked slowly up the road. His coat became heavy. He took it off and threw it over his shoulder just as he came to the spot where he thought the side-street, in which the mysterious house stood, branched off to the right. He could not go wrong. The street went down-hill but not nearly so steeply as it had seemed during the night. It was a quiet little street. There were rosebushes carefully covered with straw in a front garden, and in the next yard stood a baby carriage. A boy in a blue jersey suit was romping about and a laughing young woman watched him from a ground-floor window. Next came an empty lot, then an uncultivated fenced-in garden, then a little villa, next a lawn, and finally—there was no doubt about it—the house he was looking for. It certainly did not seem large or magnificent. It was a one-story villa in modest Empire style and obviously renovated a comparatively short time before. The green blinds were down and there was nothing to show that anyone lived there. Fridolin looked around. There was no one in the street, except farther down where two boys with books under their arms were going in the opposite direction. He stopped in front of the garden gate. And what was he to do now? Simply walk back again? That would be too ridiculous, he thought, looking for the bell-button. Supposing someone answered it, what was he to say? Well, he would simply ask if the pretty country house was to let for the summer. But the house-door had already opened and an old servant in plain morning livery came out and slowly walked down the narrow path to the gate. He held a letter in his hand and silently pushed it through the iron bars to Fridolin whose heart was beating wildly.

"For me?" he asked, hesitantly. The servant nodded, went back to the house, and the door closed behind him. What does that mean? Fridolin asked himself. Can it possibly be from her? Does she, herself, own the house? He walked back up the street quickly and it was only then that he noticed his name on the envelope in large, dignified letters. He opened it, unfolded a sheet and read the following:

> *Give up your inquiries which are perfectly useless, and consider these words a second warning. We hope, for your own good, that this will be sufficient.*

This message disappointed him in every respect, but at any rate it was different from what he had foolishly expected. Nevertheless, the tone of it was strangely reserved, even kindly, and seemed to show that the people who had sent it by no means felt secure.

Second warning—? How was that? Oh yes, he had received the first one during the night. But why *second* warning—and not the last? Did they want to try his courage once more? Was he to pass a test? And how did they know his name? Well, that wasn't difficult. They had probably forced Nachtigall to tell. And besides—he smiled at his absent-mindedness—his monogram and his full address were sewn into the lining of his fur coat.

But, though he had made no progress, the letter on the whole reassured him, just why he couldn't say. At any rate he was convinced that the woman he was so uneasy about was still alive, and that it would be possible to find her if he went about it cautiously and cleverly.

He went home, feeling rather tired but with a strange sense of security which somehow seemed deceptive. Albertina and the child had finished their dinner, but they kept him company while he ate his meal. There she sat opposite him, the woman who had calmly allowed him to be crucified the preceding night. She was sitting there with an angelic look, like a good housewife and mother, and to his surprise he did not hate her. He enjoyed his meal, being in an excited, cheerful mood, and, as he usually did, gave a very lively account of the little professional incidents of the day. He mentioned especially the gossip about the doctors, about whom he always kept Albertina well informed. He told her that the appointment of Hügelmann was as good as settled, and then spoke pf his own determination to take up scientific work again with greater energy. Albertina knew this mood. She also knew that it usually didn't last very long and betrayed her doubts by a slight smile. When Fridolin became quite warm on the subject, she gently smoothed his hair to calm him. He started slightly and turned to the child, so as to remove his forehead from the embarrassing touch. He took the little girl on his lap and was just

ARTHUR SCHNITZLER

beginning to dance her up and down, when the maid announced that several patients were waiting.

Fridolin rose with a sigh of relief, suggesting to Albertina that she and the child ought to go for a walk on such a beautiful, sunny afternoon, and went to his consulting room.

During the next two hours he had to see six old patients and two new ones. In every single case he had his whole mind on the subject. He made examinations, jotted down notes and wrote prescriptions—and he was glad that he felt so unusually fresh and clear in mind after spending the last two nights almost without sleep.

At the end of his consultation period, he stopped to see his wife and little daughter once more. He noted with satisfaction that Albertina's mother was with her, and that the child was having a French lesson with her governess. It was only when he reached the front steps that he realized that all this order, this regularity, all the security of his existence, was nothing but deception and delusion.

Although he had excused himself from his afternoon duties at the hospital, he felt irresistibly drawn to his ward. There were two cases there of special importance to the piece of research he was planning. He was busy for sometime making a more detailed study of them than he had yet done, and following that he still had to visit a patient in the heart of the city. It was already seven o'clock in the evening when he stood before the old house in Schreyvogel Strasse. As he looked up at Marianne's window, her image, which had completely faded from his mind, was revived—more clearly than that of all the others. Well—there was no chance of failure here. He could begin his work of vengeance without any special exertion and with little difficulty or danger. What might have deterred others, the betrayal of her fiancé, only made him keener. Yes, to betray, to deceive, to lie, to play a part, before Marianne, before Albertina, before the good Doctor Roediger, before the whole world. To lead a sort of double life, to be the capable, reliable physician with a future before him, the upright husband and head of a family. And at the same time a libertine, a seducer, a cynic who played with people, with men and women, just as the spirit moved him—that seemed to him, at the time, very delightful. And the most delightful part was that at some future time, long after Albertina fancied herself secure in the peacefulness of marriage and of—family life—he would confess to her, with a superior smile, all of his sins, in retribution for the bitter and shameful things she had committed against him in a dream.

On the steps he met Doctor Roediger who held out his hand cordially.

"How is Fraülein Marianne?" asked Fridolin, "is she a little more composed?"

Doctor Roediger shrugged his shoulders, "She was prepared for the end long enough, doctor.—Only when they came this noon to call for the corpse—"

"So that's already been done?"

Doctor Roediger nodded. "The funeral will be at three o'clock tomorrow afternoon."

Fridolin looked down. "I suppose—Fraülein Marianne's relatives are with her?"

"No," replied Doctor Roediger, "she is alone now. She will be pleased to see you once more, for tomorrow my mother and I are taking her to Modling." When Fridolin raised his eyes with a politely questioning look, Doctor Roediger continued: "My parents have a little house out there. Goodbye, doctor. I still have many things to attend to. It's unbelievable how much trouble is connected with such a—case. I hope I shall still find you upstairs when I return." And as he said this he reached the street.

Fridolin hesitated a moment, then slowly went up the stairs. He rang the bell and Marianne herself opened the door. She was dressed in black and had on a jet necklace which he had never seen before. Her face became slightly flushed.

"You made me wait a long time," she said, smiling feebly.

"Forgive me, Fraülein Marianne, this was a particularly busy day for me."

They passed through the death-chamber, in which the bed was now empty, into the adjoining room where, under the picture of the officer in a white uniform, he had, the day before written the

ARTHUR SCHNITZLER

death certificate of the Councilor. A little lamp was burning on the writing desk, and it was nearly dark.

Marianne offered him a seat on the black leather divan and sat down opposite him.

"I have just met Doctor Roediger. So you are going to the country tomorrow?"

Marianne seemed little surprised at the cool tone of his question and her shoulders drooped when he continued almost harshly: "I think that's very sensible." And he explained in a matter-of-fact way what a favorable effect the good air and the new environment would have on

She sat motionless, and tears streamed down her cheeks. He saw them, feeling impatient rather than sympathetic. The thought that the next minute, perhaps, she might be lying at his feet, repeating her confession of the night before, filled him with fear. When she said nothing he got up suddenly. "Much as I regret it, Fraülein Marianne—" He looked at his watch.

Still crying, she raised her head and looked at Fridolin. He would gladly have said something kind to her, but found it difficult to do so.

"I suppose you will stay in the country for several days," he began rather awkwardly. "I hope you will write to me. . . By the way, Doctor Roediger says the wedding is to be soon. Let me offer you my best wishes."

She did not move, as though she had understood neither his congratulations nor his farewell. He held out his hand but she refused it, and he repeated almost reproachfully: "Well then, I sincerely hope that you will keep me posted about your health. Goodbye, Fraülein Marianne."

She sat there as if turned to stone and he left the room, stopping for a second in the doorway, as though to give her a last opportunity to call him back. But she turned her head away, and he closed the door behind him. When he was out in the hallway he felt rather remorseful and for a moment he thought of going back, but he felt that it would have been ridiculous to do so.

But what was he to do now? Go home? Where else could he go? Anyhow, there was nothing more he could do today. And what about tomorrow? What could he do and how should he go about it? He felt awkward and helpless. Everything he put his hands to turned out a failure. Everything seemed unreal: his home, his wife, his child, his profession, and even he himself, mechanically walking along through the nocturnal streets with his thoughts roaming through space. The clock on the Rathaus tower struck half past seven. It didn't matter how late it was; he had more time on his hands than he needed. There was nothing and no one that interested him, and he pitied himself not a little. Then the idea occurred to him—not deliberately but as a flash across his mind— to drive to some station, take a train, no matter where, and to disappear, leaving everyone behind. He could then turn up again, somewhere abroad, and start a new life, as a different personality. He recalled certain strange pathological cases which he had read in books on psychiatry, so called double-lives. A man living in normal circumstances suddenly disappeared, was not heard from, returned months or years later and didn't remember where he had been during this time. Later, however, someone who had run across him, somewhere, in a foreign country, recognized him, but the man himself remembered nothing. Such things certainly didn't happen very often, but just the same they were authentic. Many others probably experienced the same things in a lesser degree. For instance, when one comes back out of dreams. Of course, one remembers some dreams, but there must be others one completely forgets, of which nothing remains but a mysterious mood, a curious numbness. Or one doesn't remember until very much later, and doesn't even then know whether it was real or only a dream. *Only* a dream!

While Fridolin wandered along, drifting aimlessly towards his home, he entered the neighborhood of the dark, rather questionable street, where he had accompanied the forlorn little girl to her humble room less than twenty-four hours before. Why was she "forlorn?" And why was just *this* street "questionable?" Isn't it strange how we are misled by words, how we give names to streets, events and people, and form judgments about them, just because we are too lazy to change our habits? Wasn't this young girl in reality the most charming, if not actually the purest of all those with whom he had come in contact during the past night? He felt rather touched when he thought of her, and remembering his plan of the night before, he turned into the nearest store and bought all kinds of delicacies. Walking along with his package, the consciousness of performing an act which was at least sensible, and perhaps actually laudable, made him feel glad. Nevertheless, he turned up his coat collar when he stepped into the hallway and went upstairs several steps at a time. The bell of the apartment rang with unwelcome shrillness and he felt relieved when a disreputable looking woman informed him that Fraülein Mizzi was not at home. But before the woman had an opportunity of taking charge of the package for Mizzi, another woman joined them. She was still young and not bad-looking, and had on a sort of bathrobe. "Whom are you looking for?" she said, "Fraülein Mizzi? Well, she won't be home again for sometime."

The older woman made a sign to her to keep quiet, but Fridolin, anxious to confirm what he had already half guessed asked very simply: "She's in the hospital, isn't she?"

"Well, as long as you know it anyhow. But there's nothing wrong with *me*, thank heaven," she exclaimed vivaciously and stepped quite close to Fridolin. Her lips were half open, and as she boldly drew up her voluptuous body the bathrobe parted. Fridolin declined and said: "I was passing by and I stopped to bring something for Mizzi." He suddenly felt very young, but asked in a matter-of-fact voice: "In which ward is she?"

The younger woman mentioned the name of a professor in whose clinic Fridolin had been an assistant several years before, and added good-naturedly: "Just let me have those packages, I'll take them to her tomorrow. And I promise that I won't snitch any of it. I'll give her your regards too and tell her that you're still true to her."

She stepped closer to him and laughed invitingly but when he drew back a little she gave it up at once and said, as if to console him: "The doctor said she'd be home in six or, at most, eight weeks."

When Fridolin returned to the street he felt choked with tears. He knew that this was not because he was deeply affected, but because his nerves were gradually giving way, and he intentionally struck up a quicker and more lively pace than he was in the mood for. Was this another and final sign that everything was bound to turn out a failure for him? But why should it? The fact that he had escaped such a great danger might just as well be a good sign. Was it the all-important thing to escape danger? He could expect to face many others, as he was by no means ready to give up the search for the marvelous woman of the night before.

Of course, it was too late to do anything about it now. Besides, he had to consider carefully just how to continue the search.

If only there were someone he could consult in the matter! But he knew of no one to whom he was willing to confide his adventures of the preceding night. For years he had not exchanged confidences with anyone except his wife, and of course, he could hardly discuss this case with her. Neither this nor any other. For, no matter how one looked at it, she had permitted him to be crucified the night before.

And he suddenly realized why he was walking, not towards his house, but, unconsciously, farther and farther in the opposite direction. He would not, and could not, face Albertina now. The most sensible tiling to do was to have supper away from home, then he could go to his ward and look after his two cases. But under no circumstances would he go home—"home?"—until he could be certain of finding Albertina asleep.

He entered a café, one of the more quiet and select ones near the Rathaus. He telephoned home not to expect him for supper, and hung up the receiver quickly so that Albertina wouldn't have a chance to come to the phone.

Then he sat down by a window and drew the curtain. A man had just taken a seat in a distant corner. He wore a dark overcoat and inconspicuous clothes and Fridolin thought he had seen his face before, during the day. It might, of course, be just a fancy. He picked up an evening paper, read a few lines here and there, just as he had done the night before in a different place. Reports on political events, articles on the theatre, art and literature, accounts of accidents and disasters. In some city that he had never heard of in the United States a theatre had burned down. Peter Korand, a chimney-sweep, had thrown himself out of a window. Somehow, it seemed strange to Fridolin that even chimney-sweeps occasionally commit suicide.

Involuntarily he wondered whether the man had first washed himself properly or whether he had plunged into nothingness just as he was, black and dirty. A woman had taken poison that morning in a fashionable hotel in the heart of the city. She was an unusually good-looking woman and had registered there a few days before under the name of Baroness D. At once Fridolin felt a strange presentiment. The woman had returned to the hotel at four o'clock in the morning, accompanied by two men who had left her at the door. Four o'clock! That was exactly the time that he, too, had reached home. About noontime—the account continued—she had been found unconscious in her bed with every indication of serious poisoning. . . An unusually good-looking woman. . . Well, there were many unusually good-looking women. . . There was no reason to believe that Baroness D., or rather the woman who had registered as such, and a certain other person, were one and the same. And yet—his heart throbbed and his hand trembled as it held the paper. In a fashionable hotel. . . which one—? Why so mysterious?—so discreet? . . ."

He put the paper down and at the same time the man in the far corner raised his, a large, illustrated journal, and held it to shield his face. Fridolin at once picked up his paper again and decided that the ". . .Baroness D. must certainly be the woman he had seen the night before. In a fashionable hotel. . . There were not many which would be considered—by a Baroness D. . . . Whatever happened now, this clue had to be followed up. He called for the waiter, paid his bill and left. At the door he turned to look for the suspicious character in the corner, but strange to say, he was already gone. . . .

Serious poisoning. . . But she was still living. . . She was living when they found her." There was really no reason to suppose that she had not been saved. In any case, he would find her—whether she lived or not. And he would see her—dead or alive. He would see her; no one in the world could stop his seeing the woman who had died on his account; who had, in fact, died for *him*. He was the cause of her death—he alone—if it were she. Yes, it was she. Returned to the hotel at four o'clock in the morning, accompanied by two men! Very likely the same men who had taken Nachtigall to the station a few hours later. This did not seem to point to a very clear conscience.

He stood in the large Square before the Rathaus and looked around. There were only a few people in sight and the suspicious looking man from the café was not among them. But even if he were—the men had been afraid—Fridolin had the upper hand. He hurried on, took a cab when he reached the Ring, and driving first to the Hotel Bristol, asked the concierge, as though he were fully authorized to do so, whether the Baroness D. who had taken poison that morning, had stopped at this hotel. The concierge didn't seem at all surprised; perhaps he thought Fridolin was a police officer or someother official. At any rate, he replied courteously that the sad case had not occurred there, but in the Hotel Erzherzog Karl. . .

Fridolin at once went there and found that Baroness D. had been taken to the General Hospital immediately after they found her. He also inquired how they had discovered her attempt at suicide. Why had they disturbed at noon a lady who had not returned until four in the morning? Well, it was quite simple; two men (the two men again!) had asked for her at eleven o'clock in the morning. The lady had not answered her telephone, although they had rung several times, and when the maid knocked on her door, there was no answer. It was locked on the inside. Finally, they had had to break it open, and they found the Baroness in her bed, unconscious. They had at once called an ambulance and notified the police.

"And the two men?" asked Fridolin, rather sharply. He felt like a detective.

Yes, of course the two men looked rather suspicious. In the meantime they had completely disappeared. Anyhow, it was unlikely that she was really the Baroness Dubieski, the name under which she had registered. This was the first time she had stopped at the hotel. Besides, there wasn't a family by that name; at least none belonging to the nobility.

Fridolin thanked the concierge for the information and left quickly, for one of the hotel managers had just come up and looked him over with unpleasant curiosity. He got back into the cab and told the cabman to take him to the hospital. A few minutes later, in the outside office, he learned that the alleged Baroness Dubieski had been taken to the second clinic for internal medicine. In spite of all the efforts of the doctors, she had died at five in the afternoon—without having regained consciousness.

Fridolin breathed a sigh of relief that sounded now like a deep groan. The official on duty looked up, startled, and Fridolin pulled himself together and courteously took his leave. A minute later he stood again outdoors. The hospital park was empty except where a nurse, in her blue and white uniform and cap, was walking along a near-by path. "She is dead," Fridolin said to himself.—If it *is* she. And if it is not? If she still lives, how can I find her?

Only too easily could Fridolin answer the question as to where at that moment he could find the body of the unknown woman. As she had died so recently, she was undoubtedly lying in the hospital morgue, a few hundred paces away. As a doctor, there would, of course, be no difficulty in gaining admittance there, even at such a late hour. But—what did he want there? He had never seen her face, only her body. He had only snatched a hasty glance at the former when he had been driven out. Up to this moment he hadn't thought of that fact. During the time since he had read the account in the paper he had pictured the suicide, whose face he didn't know, as having the features of Albertina. In fact, he now shuddered to realize that his wife had constantly been in his mind's eye as the woman he was seeking. He asked himself again why he really wanted to go to the morgue. He was sure that if he had met her again alive—whether days or years later, whatever the circumstances—he would unquestionably have recognized her by her gait, her bearing, and above all by her voice. But now he was to see only the body again, the dead body of a woman, and a face of which he remembered only the eyes, now lifeless. Yes—he knew those eyes, and the hair which had suddenly become untied and had enveloped her naked body as they had driven him from the room. Would that be enough to tell him if it were unmistakably she?

With slow and hesitating steps he crossed the familiar courtyards to the Institute of Pathological Anatomy. Finding the door unlocked, it was unnecessary to ring the bell. The stone floor resounded under his footsteps as he walked through the dimly lighted hall. A familiar, and to a certain extent homelike, smell of all kinds of chemicals pervaded the place. He knocked on the door of the Histological Room where he expected to find some assistant still at work. A rather gruff voice called "Come in." Fridolin entered the high-ceilinged room which seemed almost festively illuminated. As he half expected, Doctor Adler, an assistant in the Institute and an old fellow-student of his, was in the center of the room. He raised his eyes from the microscope and arose from his chair.

"Oh, it's you," he said to Fridolin, a little annoyed, but also surprised, "to what do I owe the honor of your visit at such an unaccustomed hour?"

"Forgive me for disturbing you," said Fridolin. "I see you are just in the midst of some work."

"Yes, I am," replied Alder in the sharp voice which he retained from his student days. He added in a lighter tone: "What else could one be doing in these sacred halls at midnight? But, of course, you're not disturbing me in the least. What can I do for you?"

When Fridolin did not answer, he continued: "That Addison case you sent down to us today is still lying over there, lovely and inviolate. Dissection tomorrow morning at eight-thirty."

With a gesture Fridolin indicated that that was not the reason of his visit. Doctor Adler went on: "Oh, then it's the pleural tumor. Well, the histological examination has unmistakably shown sarcoma. So you needn't worry about that either."

Fridolin again shook his head. "My visit has nothing to do with—official matters."

"Well, so much the better," said Adler. "I was beginning to think that your bad conscience brought you down here when all good people should be sleeping."

"It *has* something to do with a bad conscience, or at least with conscience in general," Fridolin replied.

"Oh!"

"Briefly, and to the point,"—he spoke in a dry, off-hand tone—"I should like to have some information about a woman who died of morphine poisoning in the second clinic this evening. She is likely to be down here now, a certain Baroness Dubieski." He continued more hurriedly: "I have a feeling that this so called Baroness is a person I knew casually years ago, and I am interested to know if I am right—."

"Suicidium?" asked Adler.

Fridolin nodded. "Yes, suicide," he translated, as though he wished to restore the matter to a personal plane.

Adler jokingly pointed his finger at him. "Was she unhappily in love with your Excellency?"

Fridolin was a little annoyed and answered, "The suicide of the Baroness Dubieski has nothing whatever to do with me personally."

"I beg your pardon, I didn't mean to be indiscreet. We can see for ourselves at once. As far as I know, no request from the coroner has come tonight. Very likely—"

Post-mortem examination—flashed across Fridolin's mind. That might easily be the case. Who knows whether her suicide was in any sense voluntary? He thought again of the two men who had so suddenly disappeared from the hotel after learning of her attempt at suicide. The affair might still develop into a criminal case of great importance. And mightn't he—Fridolin—perhaps be summoned as a witness?—In fact, wasn't it really his duty to report to the police?

He followed Doctor Adler across the hallway to the door opposite, which was ajar. The bare high room was dimly lighted by the low, unshaded flames of a two-armed gas-fixture. Less than half of the twelve or fourteen morgue tables were occupied by corpses. A few bodies were lying there naked. Others were covered with linen sheets. Fridolin stepped up to the first table by the door and carefully drew back the covering from the head of the corpse. A glare from Doctor Adler's flashlight suddenly fell upon it and Fridolin saw the yellow face of a gray-bearded man. He immediately covered it again with the shroud. On the next table was the naked, emaciated body of a young man, and Doctor Adler called out from farther down: "Here's a woman between sixty and seventy, so I suppose she isn't the one either."

Fridolin suddenly felt irresistibly drawn to the end of the room where the sallow body of a woman faintly glowed in the darkness. The head was hanging to one side and the long dark hair almost touched the floor. He instinctively stretched out his hand to put the head in its proper position, but feeling a certain dread which, as a doctor, was otherwise unknown to him he drew back his hand. Doctor Adler oame up and, pointing to the corpses behind him, remarked : "All those are out of the question, so it's probably this one?" He pointed his flashlight at the woman's head. Overcoming his dread, Fridolin raised it a little with his hands. A white face with halfclosed eyelids stared at him. The lower jaw hung down limply, the narrow upper lip was drawn up, revealing the bluish gums and a number of white teeth.

Fridolin could not tell whether this face had ever been beautiful, even as lately as the day before. It was a face without any expression or character. It was dead. It could just as easily have been the face of a woman of eighteen, as of thirty-eight.

"Is it she?" asked Doctor Adler.

Fridolin bent lower, as though he could, with his piercing look, wrest an answer from the rigid features. Yet at the same time he knew that if it were *her* face, and *her* eyes, the eyes that had shone at him the day before with so much passion, he would not, could not—and in reality did not, want to know. He gently laid the head back on the table. His eyes followed the moving flashlight, passing along the dead body. Was it her body?—The wonderful alluring body for which, only yesterday, he had felt such agonizing desire? Fridolin touched the forehead, the cheeks, the shoulders and arms of the dead woman, doing so as if compelled and directed by an invisible power. He twined his fingers about those of the corpse, and rigid as they were, they seemed to him to make an effort to move, to seize his hand. Indeed, he almost felt that a vague and distant look from underneath her eyelids was searching his face. He bent over her, as if magically attracted.

Suddenly he heard a voice behind him whispering: "What on earth are you doing?"

Fridolin regained his senses instantly. He freed his fingers from those of the corpse, and taking her thin wrists, placed the ice-cold arms alongside of the body very carefully, even a little scrupulously. It seemed to him that she had just at that moment died. He turned away, directed his steps to the door and across the resounding hallway back into the room which they had left a little while before. Doctor Adler followed in silence and locked the door behind them.

Fridolin stepped up to the wash-basin. "With your permission," he said and carefully washed his hands with disinfectant. Doctor Adler seemed anxious to continue his interrupted work without further ceremony. He switched on his microscope lamp, turned the micrometer screw and looked into the microscope. When Fridolin went up to him to say goodbye he was already completely absorbed.

"Would you like to have a look at this preparation?" he asked.

"Why?" asked Fridolin absentmindedly.

"Well, to quiet your conscience," replied Doctor Adler—as if he assumed that, after all, the purpose of Fridolin's visit had been a medical-scientific one.

"Can you make it out?" he asked, as Fridolin looked into the microscope. "It's a fairly new staining method."

Fridolin nodded, without raising his eyes from the glass. "Perfectly ideal," he said, "a colorful picture, one might say."

And he inquired about various details of the new technique.

Doctor Adler gave him the desired explanations. Fridolin told him that the new method would most probably be very useful to him in some work he was planning for the next few months, and asked permission to come again to get more information.

"I'm always at your service," said Doctor Adler. He accompanied Fridolin over the resounding flag-stones to the locked outer door, and opened it with his own key.

"You're not going yet?" asked Fridolin.

"Of course not," replied Doctor Adler. "These are the very best hours for work—from about midnight until morning. Then one is at least fairly certain not to be disturbed."

"Well"—said Fridolin, smiling slightly, as if he had a guilty conscience.

Doctor Adler placed his hand on Fridolin's arm reassuringly, and then asked, with some reserve: "Well—was it she?"

Fridolin hesitated for a moment, and then nodded, without saying a word. He was hardly aware that by this action he might be guilty of untruthfulness. It did not matter to him whether the woman—now lying in the hospital morgue—was the same one he had held naked in his arms twenty-four hours before, to the wild tunes of Nachtigall's playing. It was immaterial whether this corpse was someother unknown woman, a perfect stranger whom he had never seen before. Even if the woman he had sought, desired and perhaps loved for an hour were still alive, he knew that the body lying in the arched room—in the light of flickering gas-flames, a shadow among shadows, dark, without meaning or mystery as the shadows themselves—could only be to him the pale corpse of the preceding night, doomed to irrevocable decay.

VII

Fridolin hurried home through the dark and empty streets. After undressing in the consultation room, as he had done twenty-four hours before, he entered the bedroom as silently as possible.

He heard Albertina breathing quietly and regularly and saw the outlines of her head on the soft pillow. Unexpectedly, his heart was filled with a feeling of tenderness and even of security. He decided to tell her the story of the preceding night very soon—perhaps even the next day—but to tell it as though everything he had experienced had been a dream. Then, when she had fully realized the utter futility of his adventures, he would confess to her that they had been real. Real? he asked himself—and at this moment he noticed something dark quite near Albertina's face. It had definite outlines like the shadowy features of a human face, and it was lying on his pillow. For a moment his heart stopped beating, but an instant later he saw what it was, and stretching out his hand, picked up the mask he had worn the night before. He must have lost it in the morning when making up his bundle, and the maid or Albertina herself had found it. Undoubtedly Albertina, after making this find, suspected something—presumably, more and worse things than had actually happened. And she intimated this, by placing the mask on the pillow beside her, as though it signified his face, the face of her husband who had become an enigma to her. This playful, almost joking action seemed to express both a gentle warning and her readiness to forgive. Fridolin confidently hoped that, remembering her own dream, she would not be inclined to take his too seriously, no matter what might have happened. All at once, however, he reached the end of his strength. He dropped the mask, uttered a loud and painful sob—quite unexpectedly—sank down beside the bed, buried his head in the pillows, and wept.

A few minutes later he felt a soft hand caressing his hair. He looked up and from the depths of his heart he cried: "I will tell you everything."

She raised her hand, as if to stop him, but he took it and held it, and looked at her both questioningly and beseechingly. She encouraged him with a nod and he began his story.

The gray dawn was creeping in through the curtains when Fridolin finished. Albertina hadn't once interrupted him with a curious or impatient question. She probably felt that he could not, and would not, keep anything from her. She lay there quietly, with her arms folded under her head, and remained silent long after Fridolin had finished. He was lying by her side and finally bent over her, and looking into her immobile face with the large, bright eyes in which morning seemed to have dawned, he asked, in a voice of both doubt and hope: "What shall we do now, Albertina?"

She smiled, and after a minute, replied: "I think we ought to be grateful that we have come unharmed out of all our adventures, whether they were real or only a dream."

"Are you quite sure of that?" he asked.

"Just as sure as I am that the reality of one night, let alone that of a whole lifetime, is not the whole truth."

"And no dream," he said with a slight sigh, "is entirely a dream."

She took his head and pillowed it on her breast. "Now I suppose we are awake," she said,—"for a long time to come."

He was on the point of saying, "Forever," but before he could speak, she laid her finger on his lips and whispered, as if to herself: "Never inquire into the future."

So they lay silently, dozing a little, dreamlessly, close to one another—until, as on every morning at seven, there was a knock on the door; and, with the usual noises from the street, a victorious ray of light through the opening of the curtain, and the clear laughter of a child through the door, the new day began.

THE END

A Note About the Author

Arthur Schnitzler (1862–1931) was an Austrian author and dramatist. Born in the capital of the Austrian Empire, Schnitzler descended from two Jewish families, with his mother being Luise Markbreiter and his father being the well-renowned Johann Schnitzler. He would enter the practice of medicine like his father and maternal grandfather before him and begin work at Vienna's General Hospital after completing his doctorate at the University of Vienna. This career path, however, would be short-lived as over the next ten years, Schnitzler's interest in the medical field would dwindle and he would set out to make a career for himself as a writer. Beginning with his first play *Anatol* (1893), Schnitzler would go on to publish over a dozen works with the most notable being the controversial play *Reigen* (1897), the sensual novella *Rhapsody: A Dream Novel* (1926), and the socio-political novel *The Road into the Open* (1908), and become known for his frank descriptions of sexuality, commitment to writing "of love and death," and strong stance against antisemitism.

Note from the Publisher

Since our inception in 2020, Mint Editions has kept sustainability and innovation at the forefront of our mission. Each and every Mint Edition title gets a fresh, professionally typeset manuscript and a dazzling new cover, all while maintaining the integrity of the original book. With thousands of titles in our collection, we aim to spotlight diverse public domain works to help them find modern audiences. Mint Editions celebrates a breadth of literary works, curated from both canonical and overlooked classics from writers around the globe.

bookfinity & ◣ MINT EDITIONS

Enjoy more of your favorite classics with Bookfinity,
a new search and discovery experience for readers.
With Bookfinity, you can discover more vintage
literature for your collection, find your Reader Type,
track books you've read or want to read,
and add reviews to your favorite books.
Visit www.bookfinity.com, and click on
Take the Quiz to get started.

Don't forget to follow us
@bookfinityofficial and @mint_editions

Printed in the USA
CPSIA information can be obtained
at www.ICGtesting.com
LVHW011130090824
787694LV00003B/374